"I hope I didn't frighten you," the man said.

Toni glanced at his outstretched hand just as she stumbled on the top step. She reached for the handrail, missed it by inches, and would have fallen had he not caught her.

Toni shrugged free immediately and leaned against a porch pillar, embarrassed by her clumsiness and her tongue-tied reaction to the concern reflected in the man's intense blue eyes.

"Are you all right?" he asked.

Toni managed to nod. "I was just startled."

"You're trembling," he said almost accusingly. "Sit down and catch your breath."

When he put out his left hand to help her to the swing, Toni noted almost automatically that he wore no rings, adding to her suspicion that Evelyn had set up this meeting. *I don't care how good-looking he is, I won't let him rattle me,* she vowed as he sat down next to her.

"Put your head down if you feel faint," he said when Toni remained silent.

His strong features and firm chin match his forceful voice, she thought. He spoke as if accustomed to giving orders, but Toni had no intention of taking orders from him—or any other man, for that matter.

KAY CORNELIUS lives in Huntsville, Alabama, near the scenic areas described in Toni's Vow. She and her husband, Don, have two grown children and four growing grandchildren. They enjoy attending Elderhostels and serve as volunteer defensive driving instructors. Kay teaches the senior women's Bible study class in her church and likes to knit. Toni's Vow is her eighth **Heartsong Presents**.

Books By Kay Cornelius

HEARTSONG PRESENTS
HP 60—More than Conquerors
HP 87—Sign of the Bow
HP 91—Sign of the Eagle
HP 95—Sign of the Dove
HP130—A Matter of Security
HP135—Sign of the Spirit
HP206—Politically Correct

Toni's Vow

Kay Cornelius

Heartsong Presents

For Rebecca Blackwell Drake of Raymond, Mississippi, meticulous historical researcher and writer, excellent photographer, and tireless preservationist. Thank you for your generosity and encouragement—and most of all, for being my friend.

Special thanks to Mark Morrison, whose Waterfall Walks and Drives in Georgia, Alabama and Tennessee (H. F. Publishing, Inc., Douglasville, GA) is a marvelous guide to the natural beauty of DeSoto State Park and Little River Canyon National Preserve. Thanks also to Travis Overstreet of Leawood, Kansas, for his expert assistance in musical matters.

A note from the Author:
I love to hear from my readers! You may correspond with me by writing:

> **Kay Cornelius**
> **Author Relations**
> **PO Box 719**
> **Uhrichsville, OH 44683**

ISBN 1-59310-068-X

TONI'S VOW

Our mission is to publish and distribute inspirational products offering exceptional value and biblical encouragement to the masses.

All Scripture quotations are taken from the King James Version of the Bible.

one

Ten years?

Toni Schmidt frowned slightly. No, it *had* been ten years since her graduation from Rockdale High School, just over nine years since she had last lived in Rockdale—and three years since her last, brief visit. Yet here she was, on her way back to live in a town she had once despised.

Toni maneuvered her compact SUV around a slow-moving logging truck. The road to Rockdale lay somewhere ahead, and assuming that the truck was bound for the Rockdale Lumber Mill, Toni had no desire to follow it through the winding, two-lane road that had been at least partially responsible for the town's relative isolation.

In her desire to put distance between her vehicle and the truck, Toni almost missed the Rockdale turnoff and had to brake at the last minute. Gravel sprayed as the SUV's rear wheels strayed onto the shoulder. Toni slowed and straightened the vehicle, glad that no one had witnessed her screeching turn.

That wild Toni Schmidt—as reckless as ever. Toni could imagine the reaction of some of the town's gray heads. What would they think if they knew that "that awful juvenile delinquent," as Toni had once been called, was returning to the place that had once scorned her?

Toni sighed at the memory of the awkward ugly duckling she had been at fifteen. She lifted her chin to glance at her reflection in the rearview mirror. "Not that you're any great beauty now," Toni told herself aloud. Never one to dwell on her appearance, she knew that her straight mouth made her appear somewhat severe, but otherwise, her looks were unremarkable. In recent years, her light brown hair had darkened, making a pleasing contrast to her ivory skin. Her hazel eyes no longer regarded the world with fear and suspicion, but the inner wariness Toni had learned in those days hadn't entirely disappeared.

She spread the neatly manicured fingers of one hand across the steering wheel and recalled how she had once bitten her fingernails to the quick. That was just one of her many bad habits that Evelyn Trent had helped Toni change.

Toni reached the posted speed of 55 miles per hour, leaned back in the seat, and reviewed the chain of circumstances that had led her to this day. Because of E-mail and the instant accessibility of her cell phone, Toni rarely wrote or received personal letters. She checked her Atlanta post office box only a few times a week and seldom found it full. Therefore, several months ago Toni had been surprised to find two letters with a Rockdale, Alabama, postmark.

One she recognized at once; Evelyn Trent's distinctive handwriting hadn't changed since she'd served as Toni's guardian. They now kept in touch through exchanging Christmas letters— interspersed with infrequent telephone calls and E-mails—but in the first few years after Toni left Rockdale, Evelyn's letters had been an important lifeline. The other letter, with only a Rockdale post office box for its return address, Toni put aside. Fearing the worst, she opened Evelyn Trent's envelope immediately.

Toni still remembered every word of the brief note:

> *Dear Toni,*
>   *You must be wondering why I'm writing this time of the year. I enjoyed your Christmas card. You certainly seem to be busy enough, but I sense you're not completely happy in Atlanta.*
>   *I want to discuss an important matter with you. Please call me soon.*
>
> *Evelyn*

Months later, Toni still remembered how puzzled she'd felt. The note sounded nothing like Evelyn's usual letters, and Toni feared that something was seriously wrong.

Toni resolved to call Evelyn that evening, then opened the

second envelope, which contained a quite different message.

DEAR GRADUATE OF ROCKDALE HIGH

It began, screaming in capital letters.

CAN YOU BELIEVE IT HAS BEEN TEN YEARS SINCE WE
WALKED ITS HALLS? WELL, NOW IT'S TIME TO GET
TOGETHER, SO MARK YOUR CALENDARS FOR THE THIRD
WEEKEND IN JULY! A PICNIC AND DANCE AND MANY
SURPRISES ARE IN STORE AT ROCKDALE HIGH SCHOOL.
DETAILS WILL FOLLOW.

YOUR REUNION COMMITTEE

Toni smiled, recalling how she had cringed over the idea of
the reunion. *No one would notice my absence,* she had thought,
then dropped the notice into the trash receptacle.

Toni had no wish to renew any connection with Rockdale
High School. She hadn't kept in touch with the few friends
she'd had there, and she certainly didn't want to see the snobs
who had once disdained or barely tolerated her.

Toni called Evelyn that night and immediately voiced her
concern. "Are you all right?"

"Of course I am—but thanks for asking."

"Then why did you ask me to call?"

"I plan to retire this summer. I'd like for you to consider
taking my place."

At first, Toni hadn't thought Evelyn was serious. Whatever
her former guardian's age, Evelyn Trent seemed far too
young to retire from a job she so obviously enjoyed and did
so well. Even when Evelyn had made it clear that the paperwork was already in place for her to leave her office on the
first of August, Toni could not imagine replacing her mentor.
In many subsequent conversations, she told her so repeatedly.

"For one thing, I'm not licensed to do social work in
Alabama," Toni had pointed out.

"A license is just a piece of paper. You have the necessary education and experience."

Toni thought of how Evelyn had used her considerable powers to persuade Toni, almost grudgingly, to agree to pray about it. In the end, those prayers had been the deciding factor.

Recalling the hours she had spent on her knees asking the Lord to show her His will, Toni still felt a sense of awe. She hadn't experienced a heavenly vision or heard a clear voice from the clouds telling her to go to Rockdale, but over the next few weeks, several things worked together to point her in that direction. Her work duties were changing in ways that she didn't like; her apartment building was to become a co-op, and since she couldn't afford to buy her rental unit, she'd have to move. Then in the same week, two of her friends announced their engagements, further diminishing the number of singles she knew.

᠅

A month after she received Evelyn's first letter, Toni agreed to apply to the Alabama Department of Human Resources for a social worker license. Another two months of red tape, including an interview at the state DHR headquarters in Montgomery, followed before Toni received her license—and shortly after, the offer of work in the Rockdale DHR office.

Almost before she realized she had traveled that far, Toni rounded a curve and crossed the bridge over Dale Creek that marked Rockdale's city limits. The road looked pretty much the same, but Toni noticed that the bridge had been widened.

"Congressman Winter takes good care of us," Evelyn Trent had written Toni a couple of years after Jeremy Winter's election to serve his district in Washington, D.C. Jeremy's wife, April, was Toni's first—and for a long time, only—friend in Rockdale. Toni still thanked God for the kindness they had both shown her in this place then and had continued to show her since.

April Winter telephoned to express her delight that Toni was returning to Rockdale. "Wonderful news! Jeremy and I look forward to seeing you the next time we're home."

Home. Ironically, neither April nor Jeremy had been born in Rockdale, yet there was no question that they considered the old house that had been Jeremy's grandmother's to be their only real home. Toni hadn't come to the town until after her twelfth birthday, yet Rockdale was the closest thing to a hometown she'd ever known.

Toni entered the main downtown area and stopped for a traffic light near the courthouse where Jeremy Winter had persuaded a skeptical judge to allow Evelyn Trent to become Toni's guardian. A lump formed in her throat as she recalled how close she had come to being declared incorrigible and sent to reform school. What her life might have been if that had happened, Toni could only guess—but it could not have been good.

I owe Evelyn a great deal, Toni realized. That sense of debt had been at least partly responsible for her decision to return to Rockdale.

She knew it wouldn't be possible for anyone to replace Evelyn Trent.

But with God's help, I'll do my best.

It was a vow Toni intended to keep.

two

Evelyn Trent still lived in the house where she had grown up. Her much younger brother hadn't objected when their parents deeded the house to Evelyn in return for her continuing to care for them for rest of their lives.

Although Evelyn never married, like many single school-teachers, she was often called "Ms. Trent." When they first met, Toni thought Evelyn Trent was a cranky old maid, set in her ways, and interested only in her work, which seemed to involve a lot of prying into other people's lives. With no children of her own, Evelyn had surprised many people—and per-haps herself—by taking in terrible Toni Schmidt when almost everyone else in town had given up on her.

Toni remembered the sinking feeling that had hit the pit of her stomach when she realized she would be totally at the mercy of a middle-aged, rather severe-looking social worker who had the power to send her to reform school at any time. Toni had feared the worst, yet Evelyn never mistreated her, as her biological parents, two stepmothers, and a series of foster parents had all done.

Not that her life with Evelyn had been a bed of roses. Toni had to behave herself and do her share of the housework without any talking back. Confused and unhappy, Toni had no choice but to obey her guardian, to whom she could give only a grudging respect.

Toni had enjoyed living in Evelyn's house from the start, however. The modest, three-bedroom frame bungalow with its single bathroom, small kitchen, and boxlike living and dining rooms seemed palatial compared to the succession of run-down house trailers, dingy public housing, and crowded foster homes that Toni had known all her life.

Second only to having her own room, Toni loved the deep front porch, which Evelyn had made comfortable with rocking chairs and a wicker swing. She decorated it in the summer with hanging baskets of ferns and all sorts of fragrant and colorful flowers.

On this summer day, years later, when Toni parked at the curb in front of 210 Maple Street, Evelyn was in the porch swing, apparently waiting for her.

"I figured you might get here about now," Evelyn said when Toni started up the porch steps. She waved toward a wicker table bearing a frosty pitcher covered by a hand-embroidered tea towel. "I thought you might like some lemonade after that long drive."

"Thanks—that sounds good. I see you re-covered the swing," Toni added. "I like the green stripes."

Evelyn stirred the lemonade as she spoke. "Like a lot of things around here, it was time for a change."

But you haven't changed a bit, Toni would have said if she hadn't feared embarrassing Evelyn. The once faint lines in her former guardian's face had deepened since Toni's last visit, but Evelyn still didn't look nearly old enough to retire.

"Sit down," Evelyn invited after she poured their lemonade. "I remember you said you liked this front porch better than anywhere else on earth."

"As if I'd been all that many other places at that time," Toni said somewhat ruefully. "You certainly had to put up with a great deal from me."

Toni leaned forward and spoke quickly, aware that her words would embarrass Evelyn. "I hope you know how much I appreciate everything you have done—and are still doing—for me."

Evelyn's fair cheeks colored briefly, and she looked down at her glass. "I only did what I thought was needed," she said after a long moment. Then Evelyn looked at Toni in the intent way that meant she was about to say something important. "Anyway, it wasn't a one-way street. Seeing the world through your eyes made me less rigid, so we both benefited. You've made a wonderful start in your career, but now I'm concerned about your future."

"I supposed that was why you brought me back here and offered me your job. Of course, if you've second thoughts about this whole retirement thing—"

Evelyn shook her head impatiently. "Not at all. If I didn't want to retire, I wouldn't do it. And if I didn't believe you could handle the work here, you'd still be in Atlanta. But I don't want to see you put your whole life into it, as I did."

In her surprise, Toni blurted out the only thing that occurred to her. "I always thought you were happy."

Evelyn nodded. "I was—I am. I've been blessed in many ways, but I never married or had a family of my own. The older I get, the more I regret putting my work above everything else. I sense that you might make the same mistake."

Faced with this unsettling revelation, Toni scarcely knew what to say. "I don't know what you mean."

Evelyn sighed. "For too many years, work was my whole world. I was too wrapped up in it to let anyone else in. By the time I realized my mistake, it was too late. I'm afraid this old maid wasn't a very suitable role model."

Toni raised her chin in an old gesture of defiance. "I don't intend to get married," she said, more emphatically than she intended.

Evelyn laughed ruefully. "Oh, Toni, you sound like you did the first time I saw you, fifteen years old and both fists up, ready to take on the world. I kept hoping you would make a good marriage, but when year after year you wrote that you weren't seeing anyone special, I had an idea it might be on purpose."

Toni's voice was thick with emotion. "My mother's troubles began the day she met my father. I saw them end only when she finally overdosed on the drugs he brought home. I vowed then that no man would ever have the chance to mistreat me like he did her and the women he brought home afterward."

Evelyn laid her hand comfortingly on Toni's shoulder. "I know you went through some terrible things as a child, but surely you realize that marriage doesn't have to be like that. Look at April and Jeremy Winter. April had a rough start in life too, yet you've seen how happy they are."

Not liking the turn the conversation had taken, Toni tried to change it. "Yes, they are, and I'm glad. But Jeremy Winter's already taken, and I haven't met anyone half as interesting. Since you think I should marry, maybe you've already picked out a likely candidate?"

Evelyn looked embarrassed. "Of course not. I just want you to keep an open mind. As much as you enjoy your work, your life ought to be measured by more than just your job."

"You haven't 'just had a job'—it's been more like a mission. I only hope to do half as well."

Evelyn rose, signaling her readiness to drop the subject. "Of course you will, and more. In the meantime, it's good to see you on this porch again. Bring in your things and rest awhile, if you like. At six, we're having supper with some people who want to see you."

Toni's heart sank at the thought that at least one of the "people" would probably be an eligible male. It was ironic that Evelyn Trent, who always declared that she was perfectly happy living alone, had now decided that no else should.

I respect you, Evelyn, but I don't need a matchmaker. I will not be put on inspection like a hunk of meat.

Something in Evelyn's expression prevented Toni from voicing her objections. "I've had a hard week, getting ready for the move, so I hope it won't be a late evening," she said instead.

"No, this will be a relaxed supper, very informal. What you're wearing will be fine," Evelyn added before Toni could ask if she should replace her denim jumper for something more formal.

২৯

Evelyn had reserved a large table at the rear of Statum's Family Restaurant, where April Kincaid had worked as a waitress when she and Toni first met. Of all the places in Rockdale, it was providential that Toni had picked April's apartment to rob. It wasn't something she thought of often, but now, as she was greeted by Tom Statum, she wished that Evelyn had chosen another restaurant.

Still, Toni knew she had to get used to seeing people who remembered her from those days. She was an unhappy runaway the night she'd broken into April's apartment. Toni was quite certain that her past sins had been forgiven in heaven, if not by everyone in Rockdale.

"There she is!" A man with fiery red hair rose from the table and held out his arms in welcome.

"Ted! Evelyn didn't tell me you were going to be here."

"Good thing—Toni might not have come at all," Janet Brown put in as her husband and Toni exchanged a brief hug.

"Do you still direct music at Community Church?" Toni asked.

Ted nodded. "Yes, and we're still on the lookout for new talent. When Evelyn told me you were going to be here tonight, I made her invite us."

Evelyn glanced toward the door. "Here come the others."

Toni turned, fully expecting to see at least one unattached man. Instead, two women entered the restaurant.

The older one was slender, dressed and coifed to perfection. Her face was familiar, but her name escaped Toni. The other, Toni's age and a bit more than pleasingly plump, wore a bright red linen dress and smiled brightly. Toni recognized her immediately as Mary Oliver, the daughter of the judge who had appointed Evelyn as Toni's guardian.

"Mary! How good to see you," Toni said, meaning it.

"Same here. It's been way too long since you've been in Rockdale," Mary replied.

Toni turned to the other woman, who held out her hand in greeting. "Margaret Hastings. You may not remember me, but I worked in Congressman Winter's campaign."

"Of course—and didn't you become mayor when he went to Washington?"

"She did, and she's still doing a good job in that office," Evelyn answered for Margaret.

Seated between Mary Oliver and Margaret Hastings, enjoying Tom Statum's special fried chicken dinner and sweet lemon-flavored tea, Toni felt like a spectator at a tennis match as each attempted to carry on a completely different conversation with her.

Mary wanted to tell Toni all about the upcoming tenth reunion at Rockdale High, which Toni gathered she had helped put together. Mayor Margaret kept relating various problems the town faced, as if Toni might have some power to make them go away. Across the table, Ted Brown tried to tell Toni about the growth of the church and embarrassed her by going on about how much everyone would enjoy hearing her sing there again.

By the time Tom served his famous Southern pecan pie and chicory-flavored coffee, Toni's head was swimming.

"I hope you enjoyed the evening," Evelyn said as they drove home.

"Yes, it was fun. But why do I have the feeling that I was on the menu too?" Toni asked.

Evelyn laughed. "Because in a way you are. Anyone new in Rockdale, or coming back after a long absence, has to go through a few rites of initiation into small-town life. Tonight was just a sample of what's to come."

Toni groaned. "You told me how much everyone wanted to see me. You didn't warn me that they all wanted something from me as well."

"Not all do. But small-town life is a two-way street, you know," Evelyn added.

"Right now, I feel as if I'm going the wrong way on a one-way street."

Evelyn maneuvered her old sedan into the detached garage and turned off the engine. "You'll feel better after a good night's sleep," she promised.

I hope so, Toni thought, too tired to say so. Yet as weary as she was, when she said her evening prayers, Toni felt enfolded in an almost palpable sense of peace.

God means for me to be here, and He will take care of everything. Comforted by that thought, she slept.

❧

"We'll go by the office this morning," Evelyn said when Toni joined her for breakfast.

"I thought I wasn't supposed to start work until next week."

"True, but I promised the others to bring you by today, and I have to go to the courthouse on a matter that just came up. I hope you don't mind."

"No, of course not. It'll be a good learning experience."

Evelyn laughed shortly. "That's one way to put it, but after nearly thirty-five years in this work, I'm still learning, myself. Don't be discouraged if it doesn't all fall into place at first," she added.

❧

The Rockdale Department of Human Resources office occupied the lower floor of an ancient brick building on the courthouse square. Over the years, many wanted the DHR to acquire a new building, preferably on Dale Boulevard, where parking was more accessible. Funds were never available for that, and Evelyn had said she was glad because she liked the convenience of the courthouse square location. After a dilapidated furniture store behind them was razed and the site made into a parking lot, talk of moving the office had stopped.

First Toni met Anna Hastings, the mayor's blond sister-in-law, who occupied a desk in a sunny front window.

"She's officially the secretary and receptionist, but she also makes very good coffee and fills in wherever she's needed," Evelyn explained as she introduced Anna.

"I hope you're planning to work here many more years," Toni said so seriously that Anna laughed.

Edwinna Borden, the food stamps and other entitlements manager, overheard Toni's remark. She emerged from her small office next to Evelyn's and extended her hand. "More years than I'll be here," she said.

Toni had the impression Edwinna Borden was a brusque,

businesslike woman in her late forties—the kind of person she'd far rather have as a friend than an enemy. "I'm happy to meet you," Toni said, returning her firm handshake.

Edwinna nodded toward Evelyn. "Same here, but I'd be a whole lot happier if having you here didn't mean losing Evelyn. I don't know how we'll manage without her."

Neither do I, thought Toni, then dismissed the negative thought. She could do the work—Evelyn had told her so, and in a way, so had the Lord.

"Don't start that again," Evelyn said, and Toni guessed the DHR office staff shared Toni's initial surprise that Evelyn actually intended to retire.

"Any calls?" Evelyn asked Anna.

"Just the judge's secretary, wanting to make sure you'd come over this morning."

"We're on our way," Evelyn said. "Hold down the fort, ladies."

"They seem to know their business," Toni said after they left the office and crossed the street, bound for the courthouse.

"They do. Anna started working for me right after you went off to college, and Edwinna has been here about two years."

"Why didn't either of them apply for your job?"

"Anna isn't qualified, and Edwinna lacks your experience. Besides that, her son requires specialized care, so she needs regular office hours and wants no more responsibility."

"I hope they can put up with me while I learn my way around," Toni said.

"Don't worry. You'll be fine."

"The courthouse hasn't changed," Toni said as they mounted its worn stone steps.

"The doors were painted last year. Otherwise, it's the same old building."

Toni hadn't been inside the Rockdale County Courthouse in years, but even blindfolded, she would know the musty document smell that greeted her the moment she stepped over the threshold. She felt the flesh crawl on her arms as they mounted the worn wooden steps to the courtroom where Judge Oliver—Mary's father—had heard the testimony that led him to grant Evelyn Trent's petition to become Toni Schmidt's guardian.

Toni recalled how at first it seemed that she had escaped reform school only to wind up in a different kind of prison. Evelyn had cut her very little slack. As her ward, Toni attended school every day and always had a part-time job afterward. Although Toni resented the unaccustomed discipline, she soon came to like her structured life. She made good grades, and for the first time, Toni had spending money that she hadn't stolen.

"The judge is in his chambers," Evelyn said, leading Toni through the vacant courtroom to the judge's office.

It doesn't look nearly as large as it did when I was fifteen, Toni thought.

In those days, Toni had regarded Judge Wayne Oliver as an old man. Now, as he came from behind his desk to greet them, she saw that he was far from elderly. He still had the same salt-and-pepper hair and appeared to be as vigorous as ever, despite the extra pounds the years had added to his ample frame.

"Judge, you remember Toni Schmidt," Evelyn said, and from the way he looked at her, Toni knew that this was not the first time her former guardian had mentioned her to the judge.

"Of course. Nice to see you, young lady. You'll probably be involved in the case I asked Evelyn here to discuss, so it's a good thing you came along. Have a seat, ladies."

This could very well be the same chair where I sat when my own case was being discussed. Except for the age of the child, the file from which the judge read might also have been her own. Toni hadn't come into the Rockdale jurisdiction until she was fourteen, but she had already been to juvenile court in Tennessee several times before that. The little girl in this case was eight years old and was apparently being fought over by her parents. Her father had taken her out of state in violation of the divorce decree, and the mother, charging kidnapping, had sued for full custody.

"Is the child still missing?" asked Evelyn.

Judge Oliver nodded. "When she's returned to our jurisdiction, DHR will need to investigate and prepare a report for the preliminary hearing."

"What does the child want?" Toni heard herself ask, and from the way the others looked at her, immediately knew she should have remained silent.

"That is not the question, Miss Schmidt," the judge said, as if a small child had just revealed her woeful ignorance.

"It's now a criminal matter," Evelyn added. "When the child is returned, I'm sure her feelings will be taken into account."

"I see," said Toni, who did, but she had never understood why "the system" had to function as it did. *No one ever asked me what I wanted when I was that age and being beaten black-and-blue and living hand-to-mouth. If they had, it would have saved a great deal of later grief.*

The judge continued discussing the particulars of the case for a few more minutes before he rose, shook Toni's hand again, and assured her that he looked forward to working with her.

"I hope to see you again before you really retire and leave Rockdale," he told Evelyn.

"If I go. I haven't quite decided about that," she said.

❧

"You told the judge you might not leave town," Toni said as they stepped from the gloom of the courthouse into the glare of the sun. "I thought you plan to become a world traveler."

"I do, and I will, but all in good time. I'm not much for burning my bridges."

"Neither am I—although I have burned quite a few by coming back to Rockdale."

Evelyn glanced at Toni as if to make sure she spoke seriously. "That will make it easier to build new bridges here."

Evelyn stopped at the DHR office and handed Toni a key to her front door. "I had this made for you. Go on back to the house, and I'll be along as soon as I check on some things."

"Do you want me to make lunch?" Toni asked.

"No, that won't be necessary."

Evelyn entered the DHR office, and Toni stood on the sidewalk, staring after her for a moment. Evelyn almost seemed eager to get rid of her, but Toni had no idea why.

In any case, she welcomed the short walk back to Maple Street in the still-mild summer morning. Two blocks from the courthouse, she entered one of the oldest residential areas, where home owners took obvious pride in their property. Toni had forgotten, if she ever knew, the names of most of the colorful flowers that bloomed in beds, planters, and window boxes all along the way, but she enjoyed their fragrant beauty. Nothing like this ever grew around her Atlanta apartment.

She exchanged greetings with several residents who waved from their yards or porches as she passed. No one called her by name, but Toni recognized Jenny Suiter, an older woman she remembered as a notorious gossip.

Toni hadn't had any nosy neighbors in Atlanta. The few she actually knew by name were far too occupied with their own lives to worry about hers. It wouldn't be that way in Rockdale. With a small town, the bad came with the good.

Toni was still speculating about her possible reception among people like Mrs. Suiter when she turned onto Maple Street and continued to walk, head down, toward Evelyn's house. She was almost there before a glance at the front porch stopped her in her tracks.

A man occupied the wicker swing, and Toni knew he must have been watching her for some time. Transfixed, she saw him slowly unfold his long legs and stand.

Toni's mind automatically registered that at well over six feet, this man made an imposing figure. Furthermore, he was handsome. In fact, Toni couldn't remember when she had seen any man whose appearance appealed to her so instantly.

Another thought followed immediately: Evelyn was probably responsible for his presence—and Toni wanted no part of her matchmaking.

With that in mind, Toni raised her chin and started up the porch steps, grimly resolved not to smile.

three

"I hope I didn't frighten you," the man said.

Toni glanced at his outstretched hand just as she stumbled on the top step. She reached for the handrail, missed it by inches, and would have fallen had he not caught her.

Toni shrugged free immediately and leaned against a porch pillar, embarrassed by her clumsiness and her tongue-tied reaction to the concern reflected in the man's intense blue eyes.

"Are you all right?" he asked.

Toni managed to nod. "I was just startled."

"You're trembling," he said almost accusingly. "Sit down and catch your breath."

When he put out his left hand to help her to the swing, Toni noted almost automatically that he wore no rings, adding to her suspicion that Evelyn had set up this meeting. *I don't care how good-looking he is, I won't let him rattle me,* she vowed as he sat down next to her.

"Put your head down if you feel faint," he said when Toni remained silent.

His strong features and firm chin match his forceful voice, she thought. He spoke as if accustomed to giving orders, but Toni had no intention of taking orders from him—or any other man, for that matter.

"I've never fainted in my life," she said firmly. "I am not the fainting kind."

His sudden smile revealed brilliant white teeth. "I believe you, Miss. . . ?"

Nettled that he hadn't offered his name first, Toni spoke rather shortly. "Should I know you? I'm afraid we haven't met."

The man's smile faded, and for the first time, Toni felt in control. After all, she was on Evelyn Trent's front porch as an invited guest, while for all she knew, this man could be an ax murderer.

"I'm sorry." He held out his hand again, and this time his smile, although not quite so dazzling, appeared genuine. "I'm David Trent. Evelyn is my sister."

Toni knew that Evelyn had a brother, but she was certain she had never seen his picture. She wouldn't have forgotten a face like that, even as a teenager.

"And you are?" he prompted.

Toni's initial suspicion that Evelyn might be playing matchmaker grew to an irritating certainty, and she knew how she'd like to reply: *I am Toni Schmidt, single by choice, and at this moment I am planning to boil your sister in oil for pulling this trick on me.*

The girl she had once been wouldn't have hesitated to say that and more, quite loudly, but the young woman Toni had become had learned to curb her tongue. She lifted her chin and looked him straight in the eye. "I am Toni Schmidt," she said, with rather more force than necessary.

"Glad to know you." David Trent extended his hand, and Toni had no choice but to take it. She sensed he had the strength to crush it had he wished, yet his touch seemed almost tender. When he seemed in no hurry to break the contact, Toni withdrew her hand.

Looking at him more closely, Toni realized that his eyes and mouth somewhat resembled Evelyn's. However, David Trent's rugged good looks were unmistakably masculine.

In return, David leaned back in the swing and studied Toni's face, frowning as if trying to place her.

Evelyn must have told him to come today, Toni thought at first, but now she believed that either this man didn't recognize her features or her name, or else he was a great actor.

"Toni Schmidt," he repeated, then nodded as the light of understanding showed in his eyes. "Now I remember. Aren't you the girl who lived with Evelyn for awhile?"

Great! Now that he knows my name, I'm dismissed as a girl. Although Toni knew her irritation was probably both irrational and unwarranted, she made no effort to hide it.

"I was fifteen, not exactly a child, when I came to live with Evelyn. I stayed here for just over three years."

David Trent pretended to count on his fingers. "Let's see. I was in Korea when Evelyn wrote she had taken you under her wing, so that must be—what? Close to thirteen years ago?"

Toni briefly inclined her head. With the distinct feeling that she had been bested, she tried to regain an advantage. "Now that you know my name and have computed my age, it's your turn to tell about yourself—and why you've shown up on Evelyn's front porch today."

David's eyebrows lifted slightly, as if her bluntness surprised him. "You don't mince words, do you, Miss Schmidt? I wasn't trying to guess your age, but for the record, I'm single, I'm teetering on the downhill side of forty, and I'm on my sister's front porch in Rockdale because I wanted to visit her."

He spoke pleasantly, but Toni sensed that he believed her bluntness revealed a lack of manners. Rather than attempt to alter that impression, Toni pressed on, her tone almost accusing. "Evelyn didn't tell me you were coming."

He shrugged. "She's had a lot on her mind lately. She probably forgot it. Or maybe she wanted to surprise you."

He seems to be telling the truth, Toni thought. Evelyn might not have mentioned her to David, but Toni still suspected that she had somehow contrived their meeting.

"If Evelyn meant to surprise both of us, she seems to have succeeded," Toni said. "I take it you don't live around here?"

"No. I left Rockdale when I was eighteen and never came back, or wanted to, until now."

That sounds familiar—I could say the exact same thing myself. Unwilling to share anything so personal, Toni asked another question. "What kept you away all those years?"

Her question seemed to amuse David. "I presume you're not interested in a detailed resume. Let's just say that I joined the army to see the world, and in a little over twenty-one years I've pretty well done so."

The army—I was right about him, from his bearing to his close-cropped brown hair.

Toni nodded. "You look military."

David almost winced. "Is it that obvious?"

Yes, especially the way you order people around, Toni almost said. "You mentioned being in Korea when I came to live with Evelyn. I vaguely recall her mentioning she had a brother stationed overseas."

He nodded. "Not just Korea. I went to Japan, Germany, Saudi Arabia, and Kosovo. The United States Army showed this country boy a whole new world, all right."

He doesn't sound like a country boy—he doesn't even sound Southern, Toni thought. But if she said so, David Trent might think she was flirting. Toni took pride in the fact that she had never flirted with any man, and she certainly didn't intend to start with this one.

"Where are you stationed now?"

"I'm not. Like my sister, I decided it was time to retire. Since we seem to be playing twenty questions, it's your turn now. What is someone from Atlanta doing in Rockdale?"

"How do you know I'm from Atlanta?" Toni asked, suspecting Evelyn had told him so.

David jerked a thumb toward Toni's SUV, parked at the curb. "That's yours, isn't it?"

Toni nodded, and for the first time noticed the silver pickup parked behind it.

"It doesn't take much detective work to figure that a Cobb County, Georgia, license plate on a vehicle strongly suggests that its driver lives in Atlanta."

"Lived," Toni corrected. It might not be David Trent's business, but he'd soon know the whole story, anyway. "I'm going to work in the Rockdale DHR office."

David's mouth fell open. "You're going to take my sister's place? I had no idea—that's quite amazing."

Toni looked down at her hands. "Evelyn is an amazing woman. No one who takes that job can ever replace her."

"Maybe not, but I'm sure you'll give it a good shot."

Rattled by the hint of admiration in David's voice, Toni rose abruptly. "Evelyn should be back any minute. I'll unlock the door so you can wait inside."

"Thanks. I want to get something from my truck first."

Toni watched David stride from the porch and idly noted that his full-sized pickup had four doors. Big man, big truck, she supposed. He took a package wrapped in brown paper from the passenger side of the front seat and returned to the porch.

Toni put Evelyn's house key into the lock and jiggled it several times before the door finally opened.

"That lock seems to be balky," David said. "I'll fix it while I'm here, if Evelyn will let me."

A voice behind them startled both Toni and David.

"What is it I'm supposed to let you do?" Evelyn asked, apparently trying to sound cross.

David turned to Evelyn and smiled. "Lots of things I didn't know how to do when I lived here, big sister."

Evelyn turned to Toni. "I'd introduce you, but you seem to have met."

Yes, thanks to you.

"You've been holding out on me," David said accusingly.

"Not really. Don't stand there with the door open. I can't afford to air condition the whole town. Let's go inside. How are things in Virginia? Did you have a good trip down?"

As David assured his sister that all was well, Toni wondered if his home was now in Virginia or whether he'd been visiting someone there.

I know very little about David Trent, after all, was her first thought. The second—that he intrigued her more than any other man she'd met—Toni quickly suppressed.

He's Evelyn's brother. He's come for a visit, then he'll be gone.

Toni set her lips in a grim line. She didn't have a man in her life now, and she wanted it that way.

I don't care how handsome he is. I won't let David Trent manipulate my feelings—and that's a vow.

four

David stopped in the middle of the living room and looked around. "I see you got rid of the flowered wallpaper. Otherwise, everything looks about the same."

"You haven't seen the sunroom. Ed Larkins enclosed the back porch last year. Toni, pour some lemonade for yourself and David. You two can chat in the sunroom while I get lunch together."

Evelyn pointed toward the sunroom on her way to the kitchen. David inspected the new addition and entered the kitchen, nodding his approval.

"Looks like Ed did a great building job, and you've got it decorated like something in one of those fancy magazines."

"I'm sure you read lots of those," Evelyn said, her dry tone not masking her obvious pleasure at his approval.

David took the lemonade from Toni, and Toni set her glass on the table. "You can drink it in the sunroom in peace—I'll help Evelyn," she said.

Your lemonade trap didn't work, Evelyn. Toni smiled at the thought, then quickly changed her expression when Evelyn looked annoyed.

"I've managed this kitchen just fine without you for going on ten years now. If I needed your help, I'd ask."

Toni washed her hands and dried them on a paper towel before replying. "Actually, I have fond memories of the time we spent in this kitchen."

Evelyn chuckled. "Even when you tried hard not to help?"

"Only at first, when I didn't want to admit that I didn't know how to do anything in a kitchen. You changed that in a hurry, though."

Evelyn set a bowl of potato salad on the table. " 'Slave labor,'

I think you muttered under your breath a few times."

Toni laughed. "Probably many more times than you knew."

Evelyn removed a platter of cold cuts from the refrigerator and pointed to a plastic-wrapped relish tray. "There's lettuce in the crisper, ready to go on the tray. I'll put out the bread, then we can eat. David's probably hungry."

"From all this food, you must have known he was coming today."

Evelyn turned away and busied herself with the bread. "Not really. Anyway, I couldn't let you go hungry. Tell David lunch is ready."

Toni turned to find David standing in the kitchen doorway, holding out his glass. "How about a refill? I don't know when I've had such delicious, homemade lemonade."

"My, you're full of flattery today," Evelyn said dryly. "The pitcher's on the table—help yourself. Lunch is ready."

"Where do you want me to sit?" David asked.

Evelyn looked surprised. "Why, at your usual place," she said, as if it had been days rather than years since they'd shared a meal in this kitchen.

David looked approvingly at the table. "You outdid yourself, Evelyn."

He made a move toward the potato salad bowl, then stopped when he saw his sister's folded hands.

"Sorry," he murmured.

"This isn't a mess hall," Evelyn reminded him. "Will you return our thanks?"

Toni read David's expression to mean that he didn't really want to, but he nodded, bowed his head, and mumbled a brief, formulaic grace.

"It must be hard to realize that you're a civilian again, after all these years," Toni said in the ensuing silence.

"It hasn't quite sunk in yet," David admitted. "Right now, I feel a little guilty, almost as if I'm AWOL."

"Absent without leave?" asked Toni.

"Yes. I never had that on my record, although I came close

on my first tour in Germany. I went on leave to the salt mines at Salzburg and missed my ride back to base. I almost lost a stripe before I got that straightened out."

Evelyn turned to Toni. "David was already a two-stripe sergeant by then, one of the youngest in the army." She looked back at him. "He retired with the highest enlisted rank."

David shrugged. "I was one of many sergeants major serving at brigade level."

"Tell Toni about some of the interesting places you've been," Evelyn prompted.

David's glance at Toni confirmed that he thought Evelyn was making far too much of his military career. "She already knows. We covered all of that before you got home."

Evelyn seemed pleased. "I'm glad you had the chance to get acquainted. I can't tell you how much it means to have you both under my roof again."

"I'm happy to see you too, Sis, but I'm not staying under your roof," David said.

Evelyn frowned. "Why ever not? I can make up the day bed in your old bedroom. It'll be just like when you lived here as a boy."

David shook his head. "No, thanks. Everyone will be more comfortable with me at the Rockdale Inn."

Evelyn sighed. "I see that you're still stubborn as ever. At least tell me how long you plan to stay."

"I just got here and you're already talking about getting rid of me," David complained.

"No chance of that," Evelyn said. "You never stay long enough to wear out your welcome."

Listening to them, Toni felt a pang of envy at the obvious love they shared. Her chaotic childhood had been a universe away from the normal family life which Evelyn and David took for granted, and for which Toni had longed in vain. She never had a chance to bond with the assorted foster and stepchildren with whom she had briefly lived. She rarely saw happy families then, and even when she had finally found a measure of peace with Evelyn Trent, it wasn't like being in a real family.

David finished eating and stood. "I'll be right back." He returned shortly to hand Evelyn the package Toni had seen him take from his truck. "I thought this might come in handy in a few weeks."

Evelyn removed the brown paper, revealing bright wrapping paper. "For your retirement days," she read from the card. "It's too small to be a rocking chair and too big to be a gold watch," Evelyn observed. "What can it be?"

"Open it and you'll see," urged David.

Carefully, Evelyn withdrew a hand-tooled burgundy leather travel diary and matching passport cover, both with her name embossed in gold. "Oh! I've never had anything with my name on it."

"I know you like to keep records. The travel diary has all kinds of maps and information about time zones and currency and common words and phrases in fifteen languages. I think it'll come in handy."

Evelyn smiled ruefully. "It looks as if you're determined to get me out of the country."

"You always said you want to travel," David pointed out. "Now that you have the opportunity, I hope you'll do it."

In the silence that followed, Toni recalled something Evelyn had told her years before. *I always wanted to see what lay beyond these mountains, but my responsibilities kept me here. I suppose it's just as well.*

"Thank you," Evelyn finally managed to say. "It's a beautiful gift. You'll have to help me plan my first trip."

"Gladly. Just say the word."

As if remembering Toni, Evelyn turned to her with an expression that seemed to say, *Isn't my brother wonderful?*

"It seems I'll have to travel now," she said.

"And you can certainly do so in style," Toni remarked.

David stood and stretched. "Speaking of traveling, I'll go on to the inn now and grab a shower. When should I come back to take you ladies to dinner?"

Evelyn sighed. "There's not a reason in the world that you can't stay here. He won't put us out, will he, Toni?"

It would definitely be awkward sharing one tiny bathroom with a strange man—Evelyn's brother or not.

Toni addressed David with as much sincerity as she could muster. "No, of course not. After all, this is your home. Evelyn will be disappointed if you don't accept."

David looked at Toni, his expression suggesting that he both knew and shared her true feelings about the matter. "You're both kind, but my mind's made up, and as my sister will tell you, it's not easily changed."

"So I gathered," Toni murmured, relieved that David Trent wouldn't be intimately involved in her daily life.

"All right, if you must. Come back around five-thirty," Evelyn said.

"Yes, Ma'am. And good-bye, Miss Schmidt. Nice to meet you."

"Same here," Toni said to his back as he and Evelyn went outside.

From the living room, Toni saw them standing beside his truck, engaging in an apparently serious conversation.

She's probably telling him I'm a perfect match for him, Toni thought, although she hoped it wasn't so. A man was the last thing Toni needed, particularly now.

The telephone rang, and Toni went into the hall and picked up the old-fashioned receiver. "Trent residence," she said, as Evelyn had taught her so many years ago.

"Toni, is that you? This is Ted Brown. I know it's short notice, but I hope you'll sing for us this Sunday."

Picturing the redheaded minister of music who had first encouraged her to sing in public, Toni smiled. "I've scarcely unpacked my bags."

"I know, but Janet wants you to come about eleven-thirty tomorrow for lunch. We can rehearse afterward."

Toni hesitated. She might not have been so quick to accept Ted's invitation, but it would keep her from being stuck with David Trent, at least for a few hours.

"All right, Ted. Tell me where you live now."

Evelyn returned as she hung up the phone. "Who was that?"

"Ted Brown. I agreed to have lunch with him and Janet tomorrow, if that's all right."

"Of course, but I wanted to show you and David around, so you can see what's changed in the last few years. We could pack a picnic lunch and make a day of it."

"I'll take a rain check. Maybe you should give David the tour tomorrow, since he probably won't be here very long."

Evelyn sighed. "David hasn't said when he's leaving, but I hope to persuade him to stay awhile."

Toni quickly changed the subject. "Ted wants me to sing on Sunday morning, so after lunch we'll go to the church to rehearse. I'll probably be gone all afternoon."

"I'll plan something special for tomorrow night," Evelyn said. "I'd better call Edith and see if she can do my hair this afternoon. Do you want me to make you an appointment?"

"No, thanks," she said, wondering whether Evelyn thought she should look more glamorous to suit David's tastes. "My last trim will do for a few more weeks."

Evelyn went to the telephone, and Toni returned to the kitchen to clear away the lunch dishes. As she worked, she thought how natural it seemed to be back in this house, how easily she had fallen back into their old routine.

If it weren't for David Trent, it would really be like old times. But his rather disturbing presence threatened to change everything.

Nothing is going to happen, Toni assured herself. She had no interest in David, and she suspected he wasn't overly impressed with her, either, despite what Evelyn might hope.

❧

Toni and Evelyn were sitting in the porch swing when David pulled up in his truck five-thirty on the dot. In neat tan slacks, an apparently new cotton shirt, and polished loafers, he looked even more handsome than he had that morning.

I'll give him that, Toni thought grudgingly. Never swayed

by anyone's outward appearance, she was prepared to ignore his good looks.

"Right on time," Evelyn said approvingly.

David nodded. "It didn't take too long for the army to persuade me to be prompt. I see you're ready—where shall we go?"

"How about Statum's? The food's good, and it's close."

David shrugged. "It's all right, but I wanted to take you somewhere fancier. I had the restaurant at DeSoto State Park in mind."

"We'll do that some other time." Evelyn held out the keys to her aging sedan. "We can go in my car."

David ignored her outstretched hand. "According to the ads, four adults can ride in my truck in perfect comfort. I said I'd pick you up. That means I will also drive."

"Let him," Toni said quickly. "I can't go with you, anyway. I have to call some people in Atlanta I can't reach during the day."

"Surely that can wait," Evelyn said.

"No, I don't want to put it off," Toni said. "Besides, I'm sure you and David could use some time to yourselves."

"Sorry you can't join us," David said, but what Toni read in his eyes confirmed that he probably had no more interest in his sister's matchmaking than did Toni.

Evelyn pocketed her car keys and shrugged. "All right, if you insist." To Toni she said, "We'll bring you something."

"No, thanks. I'm not really hungry—I'll have the lunch leftovers later. You'd better hurry or Statum's will be filled up."

"That's true," Evelyn agreed. "Come on, David. I guess we know when we're not wanted."

"See you later," David called over his shoulder as he and Evelyn started down the porch steps.

Not if I see you first, Buster.

Wondering why she was unaccountably rankled by the man, Toni suppressed the flip remark and waved good-bye instead.

Just ignore him, and he'll soon go away.

But as David opened the truck door for his sister, Toni knew that might be easier said than done.

five

Toni expected David Trent to come to the house for breakfast the next morning, but Evelyn said he had taken his truck to Ft. Payne for service. "He probably won't be back for hours. It's just as well, since I'll be busy nearly all day myself."

I should have saved the lunch date with Ted and Janet for another day, Toni thought. However, since she had promised to sing on Sunday, she needed to rehearse with them today.

"I don't know when I'll be home," Toni said, "but I'll have my cell phone on if you need to reach me."

Evelyn looked amused. "I recall you once fought leaving a phone number when you went out."

"I fought a lot of things, but eventually, I realized your rules had good reasons behind them."

"Maybe I had too many rules, but I always tried to do what I thought best for you."

Toni spoke lightly. "I suppose it worked. Here I am, all grown up and not in jail, and you're about to go out and see the world."

"Not quite. I'm not officially retired yet. In fact, I have to stop by the office this morning."

"Want me to go with you?" Toni asked.

"No, thanks. You'll be working there soon enough. Enjoy your freedom while you can."

❧

Later, as she drove to Ted and Janet's apartment, Toni thought it ironic that Evelyn would, on the one hand, encourage her to marry, while on the other say she should enjoy her freedom. For Toni's mother, marriage had meant the end of both her freedom and her life. Toni wanted no part of that for herself.

If freedom means doing work I enjoy, then I am already free.

And I intend to leave well enough alone.

Her route took Toni past Rockdale High School, the site of a great deal of activity. The campus message board proclaimed the reason:

WELCOME, TENTH REUNION ALUMNI

Of course—at Statum's Restaurant Mary Oliver had urged Toni to attend the reunion, even though she hadn't registered or paid for the events. Toni hadn't given Mary a definite answer, but now, attending the reunion seemed like an attractive alternative to being with David Trent.

I'll call Mary this afternoon.

Ted and Janet Brown lived on the second floor of a large brick apartment complex nestled into the base of Warren Mountain near the church where Ted led the music ministry.

Janet opened the door to Toni's knock and greeted her warmly. "I'm so glad you could come."

Toni surveyed the spacious living area dominated by Janet's grand piano. "What a lovely room!"

"It's also our studio," Ted said. "Janet gives piano lesson,s and I have a few voice students."

"Do you still play for church services?" Toni asked Janet.

"Yes, but we've gone high-tech. You won't believe our new sound system."

Over lunch, Ted and Janet updated Toni on Community Church news, then made her the topic of conversation.

"We're surprised that you haven't married yet."

"Why 'yet'?" Toni asked, nettled by Janet's presumption that she would marry.

Janet looked surprised. "With so much to bring to a marriage, it seems some nice man would have claimed you by now."

Toni didn't try to hide her annoyance. "I don't need to be 'claimed,' thank you. My life is quite full enough as it is."

Ted and Janet regarded Toni with a mixture of sadness and pity, as if she'd just said she had a fatal disease. "You may think that now, but isn't it possible that God has already chosen the perfect partner for you?" asked Ted.

"If so, He hasn't shared that information with me," Toni said. The moment the words left her lips, she realized how flip they sounded and tried to make amends. "What I mean is that a long time ago certain circumstances convinced me that marriage isn't for me. I pray to know and stay in God's will. I believe He intended for me to return to Rockdale, but that's as far as I've been led."

"We don't mean to sound critical," Janet said. "Our marriage has been so fulfilling, we want the same for you."

"That's right. At least keep all your options open," Ted urged. "When your own will is so strong about something, it's hard for God to get through with any other message."

"Not that we'd presume to tell you what to do, of course." Janet spoke so earnestly that Toni smiled.

"Of course you wouldn't. Except that Ted has presumed to tell me I'm to sing on Sunday," she teased.

Ted seemed relieved Toni had shifted the conversation to safer ground. "You are, and we need to rehearse. If you didn't bring any of your own tapes with you, I have some at the church I'd like you to hear."

"Can't Janet accompany me on the piano?" Toni asked.

"She can, but tapes with background vocals often work better with a voice like yours."

"If that's a polite way of saying I don't sing loud enough, I can raise the volume," Toni quipped.

"We'll try it both ways," Ted suggested. "Let's go."

੩੦

The moment Toni stepped inside the cool dimness of the Community Church sanctuary, she felt a strong sense of homecoming. She recalled how April Kincaid had almost literally dragged her to her first Sunday morning service so many years ago. In this place, she had accepted Christ as her Savior. And here, April, the best soprano in the choir, had encouraged Toni to join her in a shaky duet.

"Do you remember the first time you sang here?" Ted asked.

"I'll never forget it. I was trembling so much, April had to hold me up, or I know I would have fallen. We sang 'Whispering Hope' and somehow the Lord got us both through it."

"He has a way of doing that," Ted said. He was silent for a moment, then pointed to the upper rear of the sanctuary. "The new sound booth is up there. Come on, I'll show you around."

❧

By the time they had chosen a background tape and rehearsed it a few times, it was almost five o'clock. When Toni returned to Evelyn's, David's truck was nowhere in sight, and Evelyn wasn't in the house. She had left Toni a note on the telephone message board, however.

Dinner out at six. Wear something nice.

Toni sighed. She didn't look forward to an evening she suspected had been engineered to bring her and David together. However, she had no plausible excuse to stay home.

The telephone rang, and when she answered she heard Mary Oliver's lilting voice.

"Hi, Toni! I've been so busy, this is the first chance I've had to call. I hope you're coming to the reunion tomorrow."

"I meant to call you about that," Toni said. "I never sent any money—"

"I told you the other night that doesn't matter," Mary interrupted. "We're meeting in the auditorium at ten, followed by a picnic. The banquet's tomorrow night. Everyone on the committee is dying to see you."

I'm sure they are, Toni thought dryly.

"I can't make the banquet, but I suppose I could come to the morning meeting and stay for the picnic," Toni said.

"Great! Do you need a ride?"

Toni smiled, remembering the times Mary had taken her places in their teen years. "No, thanks. I'll see you at school at ten."

Toni showered and dressed in the beige linen two-piece dress she called her "uniform," suitable to wear almost anywhere. By then, it was nearly a quarter of six, and Evelyn still hadn't come home. She'd said she was going to the hairdresser's in the afternoon. She must have had some other errands to be this late.

Toni had just settled into a comfortable chair in the sunroom with the weekly Rockdale Record when the front door opened and she heard Evelyn and David talking.

Toni joined them in the living room in time to hear Evelyn say, "I'm sorry, but you'll have to go to dinner without me."

"If your head is hurting that much, maybe you should go to the emergency room," David said.

"What's happening?" asked Toni.

Evelyn turned, her face contorted with pain. "I have a headache, that's all. If I don't lie down and stay in the dark, it could turn into a nasty migraine."

"You're still having those?" Toni asked, concerned about Evelyn and fearing she would have to dine with David alone.

Evelyn shrugged. "I don't have as many bad headaches as I once did. I have pills to take for it, but the best medicine includes rest in a quiet, dark place."

"I don't think we should go off and leave you here alone," David said.

"That's exactly what I need, however," Evelyn insisted. "Don't worry about me. The dinner reservation at the country club is for six o'clock. Run along now."

&

"By my watch we're already late," David said when they left the house.

"The country club isn't likely to be overrun on a Friday night. I doubt they gave away the reservation," she said, half hoping they had.

"I haven't been in this place since my senior prom," David said a few minutes later when they entered the stone and cedar foyer of the Rockdale Country Club.

"I didn't go to my prom," Toni said, then wanted to bite her tongue. She had no intention of discussing her personal life with David Trent, and she was glad when the pert, young hostess distracted his attention.

The girl looked at David as if Toni didn't exist and smiled. "Dinner for two?" she all but purred.

"Actually, Evelyn Trent made a reservation for three, but it'll just be the two of us this evening."

The hostess made a mark on her list and called a waiter. "The special lakeside table, please." To David she added, "Enjoy your dinner."

The waiter led them to a table overlooking a small lake, which shimmered in the moonlight. Tucked away in an alcove, their table was hidden from other diners.

"Very cozy," David remarked when the waiter left.

And very romantic. Toni wondered if Evelyn had arranged that, as well.

"It's also very dark in this corner," she remarked. "How are we supposed to read the menu?"

"We don't need to. Evelyn told me that prime rib is the Friday night special. Will that suit you?"

"I've never been picky about what I eat," Toni said, immediately wishing she hadn't. *I sound like an idiot,* she thought, then wondered why she cared.

"I'm not picky either. I can thank the army for that. You wouldn't believe what I've had to eat over the years."

"Are K rations as bad as their reputation?"

"It's MREs now—meals ready to eat. Some aren't bad. All are light years better than my first army meal."

Toni relaxed a bit, glad to find a safe topic of conversation. "That sounds like a story that needs telling."

"Are you sure? I wouldn't want to spoil your appetite."

"You won't."

"All right. When I joined the army, several of us from Alabama rode from daylight into dark on an uncomfortable olive drab school bus. We finally got to Ft. Jackson about ten o'clock and the bus stopped at a mess hall. Everyone was tired and we were all hungry, at least until we saw the food."

David stopped when the waiter appeared to take their order.

After assuring them that the prime rib special was an excellent choice, he bowed and departed.

"So what was it?"

"Think of the worst food you can imagine," David invited.

"I don't care much for dried fish or anchovies."

"This was much worse. Everything was either cold, straight from the walk-in coolers, or room temperature. Green beans from a can; greasy, stiff French fries; and the entrée was," he said, pausing for effect, "cold fried liver."

Toni smiled, then found herself laughing as David continued to relate more stories about army life, and finally dismissed her suspicion that Evelyn had contrived this private dinner. When David asked her about her life in Atlanta, he appeared to be entertained by her stories as well.

Unlike the army food David described, their prime rib dinner was perfection. By the time they finished a final cup of coffee, Toni realized that the evening had turned out to be a rather pleasant diversion.

However, on the drive back to Evelyn's, David's mood sobered, and he expressed concern for his sister's health.

"Evelyn has worked hard all her life. She deserves a happy retirement. Now I wonder if her health will let her enjoy it."

"I think she's perfectly well. She's had occasional headaches ever since I've known her. They never last long."

"I still think she should see a doctor."

"She probably won't want to."

"I know, but I can outstubborn my sister if push comes to shove."

David pulled up to the curb and turned off the ignition. As he had done at the country club, he came around to open her door and help her from the truck. *David Trent has good manners—I'll give him that.*

"Would you check on Evelyn and let me know how she's doing?" David asked when they reached the front door.

"I suspect she's asleep, but I'll look in on her."

Moments later she returned; the soft snores issuing from

Evelyn's bedroom had assured Toni her assumption was correct.

"Everything's fine."

"That's good. Tell Evelyn she missed a great dinner. I don't know when I've laughed like that. You're good company, Miss Toni Schmidt."

So are you. Toni almost voiced the words. "Good night, Sergeant Major Trent," she said instead.

"Just David," he corrected.

"And Toni," she added.

With a wave, he was gone, and Toni went back into the dark house, almost sorry she had enjoyed herself so much.

Toni cast a glance at Evelyn's door and sighed. Why, she wondered, did David Trent have to come to Rockdale and complicate things?

And what, if anything, did Evelyn have to do with it?

six

As Toni expected he would, David rang Evelyn's doorbell just after breakfast.

"How's the patient?" he asked when Toni answered the door.

"Having coffee in the sunroom. Come on back."

Evelyn greeted David with a smile. "As you can see, I'm fine. All I needed was a little rest."

"What about those dark circles under your eyes?"

"With a touch of makeup, they'll be gone. Have you had breakfast?"

"Yes, but if you're offering, I'll take a cup of coffee."

"I'll get it," Toni said. "Black, no sugar."

Evelyn raised her eyebrows. "Now how did you know that?"

Toni groaned inwardly. Why did she always say too much when David Trent was around?

"We had coffee after a very good dinner last night," David answered for her. "I'm sorry you missed it."

"So am I, but Toni tells me you did just fine without me."

❧

When Toni returned with his coffee, David was telling Evelyn he had something to see to that morning.

"Come back and have lunch with me afterward," Evelyn invited. "Toni has other fish to fry today."

David glanced at Toni. "I see you're dressed up. What's the occasion?"

Toni had chosen her navy slacks and a red, white, and blue knit top with the reunion picnic in mind; the outfit was hardly "dressy," even by Rockdale standards. Obviously, David Trent had a limited knowledge of women's fashion.

"My Rockdale class is having a reunion this morning."

"I never went to any of mine," David said. "I suppose it

41

might be worth it to see how old everyone else looks."

"This is my first reunion—and likely it will be the last." Toni glanced at her watch and stood. "I should be on my way. Don't overdo yourself," she warned Evelyn.

Evelyn sounded irritated. "I told you I'm fine. You all don't need to treat me like an invalid."

"I'll be right back," David told his sister. When they reached the front porch, he asked Toni what she really thought about Evelyn's health.

Toni hesitated. She wasn't about to share her renewed suspicion about the true cause of his sister's indisposition. "Evelyn says she feels well, and I believe her."

David sighed. "I hope you're right."

He looks troubled, Toni thought as he turned away. She had noticed the lingering sadness in his eyes, even when he smiled. David hadn't mentioned the dark side of his army service, but Toni presumed he must have had his share of trauma over the years.

That's another thing we have in common. But Toni would never tell him so.

ia

"Toni! Over here!" Mary called when Toni reached the front entrance of Rockdale High. "Come in and register. I saved a seat for you in the auditorium."

Toni followed Mary to a table in the front hall, where a slightly familiar bleached blond presided over the check-in. Betty Simpson Lewis, according to her name tag.

"You remember Toni Schmidt, don't you, Betty?"

She glanced at Toni without interest. "Sure. Do you have a married name?"

"No, she doesn't. Toni and I are the only girls from our class who have never been married," Mary said for her.

Betty handed Toni her name tag and a copy of the class roster. "You never been married yet," she said. "Y'all still have plenty of time to find yourselves a man."

"If we were looking," Mary said shortly. "Come on, Toni."

"Everybody around here seems to think a single woman must want a husband," Toni said.

"Tell me about it! I don't know why they think we won't be happy until we have that M R S in front of our names."

"Maybe misery loves company," Toni said.

The auditorium was noisy with the squeals of recognition and drone of dozens of simultaneous conversations. It was already ten o'clock, but almost no one was seated.

Mary stopped near the front and pointed to a chair with its seat turned up. "I saved this place for you. I have to be on the stage, but I'll see you after the program."

Toni glanced around. The auditorium was bright with fresh paint, but the wooden seats were as uncomfortable as she remembered. As had been the case in her student days, everyone else seemed to be having a good time talking with friends, while Toni sat alone and told herself she should never have agreed to come.

While Toni waited for the program to begin, she skimmed the class listings to see what had happened to the other graduates in her class. Two were deceased, several served in the armed forces, and six hadn't been located. Some lived as far away as California and Alaska, but a surprisingly large number had stayed in or near Rockdale.

"Hello, Toni. I hoped I'd see you here."

Toni turned toward the speaker, a tall brunette whose periwinkle blue linen pantsuit set off her slender figure, and recognized Joan Bell Timmons, a former English teacher who now lived in Atlanta.

"I almost didn't come," Toni confessed. "Sit down. Do the teachers come to this reunion thing every year too?"

"No. This is the first class to invite me."

Earl Hurley, the master of ceremonies, came to the microphone and quieted the crowd. "The Rockdale ROTC color guard will now present the colors. Please rise and remain standing for the invocation."

Toni glanced at her program. Earl Hurley, son of the

Community Church pastor and the first boy she ever dated, was now Rockdale's police chief. However, his prayer of invocation indicated that he could easily have followed his father's footsteps into the ministry.

Earl then introduced the reunion committee, which included his wife, Audra, the daughter of the former Rockdale High principal. Audra had led the "in" crowd, a clique whose members delighted in making outsiders like Toni miserable.

Loud applause greeted Mary Oliver's introduction; evidently she was a great deal more popular now than back in high school, when she had been teased about her weight.

After everyone on the stage had been acknowledged, Earl pointed to the rear of the auditorium. "They wouldn't join us on the stage, but there's somebody else here I'm sure you all want to see. Congressman Jeremy Winter, you and your wife come on down!"

To laughter, applause, and a standing ovation, Jeremy and April Winter made their way down the aisle, frequently slowed by well-wishers.

Toni felt rare tears gather behind her eyelids at the unexpected sight of her first and oldest friends.

"He just gets better-looking every year," Joan murmured as Jeremy and April stood on the stage.

Toni knew Joan Bell had wanted her father's young law partner for herself. Instead, Jeremy Winter fell in love with April Kincaid, whom he met while representing Toni before Judge Oliver. After helping elect Jeremy as mayor of Rockdale, Joan met and married a prominent Atlanta neurosurgeon. A few years ago, she had been instrumental in hiring Toni to work in the nonprofit agency on whose board she sat.

Small world, Joan had said to Toni then.

Too small at times, it seemed to Toni. Especially in Rockdale, with its closed network of friends and relatives.

❧

The picnic turned out to be far more enjoyable than Toni had expected. She was pleasantly surprised that so many of the classmates who had shunned or ignored her in the past now made it a point to welcome her back to Rockdale. Once Jeremy and April sat down at the table with her and Mary, so many people came by to speak to the congressman that Toni had no chance to talk to her old friends.

"I wish Jeremy and I didn't have to be in Ft. Payne this afternoon," April told Toni. "We have so much to catch up on."

"Maybe we could meet somewhere for dinner tonight," Toni suggested.

"We're eating at home for a change. Come over about six," April invited, and Toni agreed.

Jeremy glanced at his watch and stood. "Mary, that was great barbecue. Thanks for inviting us."

Mary looked disappointed. "Do you have to go so soon? I thought maybe you'd want to address your constituents."

Jeremy laughed. "I want to make a speech even less than these folks want to hear one. I have a speech to deliver in Ft. Payne, though, and if we don't leave now, we'll be late."

"There goes a really happy couple," Mary said in the silence following their departure. "Maybe some marriages really are made in heaven."

"The trouble is, they have to be lived on earth," Toni said.

≈

Toni stayed to help the reunion committee clean up and returned to Evelyn's around four o'clock. Toni had half expected David to be there, and she was strangely disappointed not to see his truck.

She found Evelyn peeling potatoes in the kitchen, which was fragrant with the aroma of roasting meat.

"You're cooking?"

"Don't sound so surprised—I haven't forgotten how. I thought David would like a home-cooked meal tonight."

"Where is he?" Toni asked, then immediately regretted the show of interest.

"I'm not sure, but he'll be here for supper."

"I won't be, though. I saw April and Jeremy Winter at the

reunion and April invited me to supper at their house. It's been ages since we've had a long visit."

"If I'd known the Winters were in town, I could have invited them to join us here tonight."

Toni smiled. "Their twin boys are almost six. It's better for me to go there."

"All right, but David and I will miss you," Evelyn said.

Sure. He'll miss me about as much as a toothache.

Or would he?

❧

Toni hadn't seen April for several years, but the moment she walked into the old Warren house, it was as if they'd never been apart.

"You look great," April told Toni. "Could it be you're in love at long last?"

"Hardly," Toni said tartly. "You know how I feel about that."

"I know how much you were hurting when we met, but your life is so different now, I hoped you had changed your mind about marriage."

"I haven't. Where are the boys?"

"In the kitchen with Gladys. You'll see them soon enough."

"I'm glad you still have her," Toni said, remembering the older woman Jeremy had hired to help April when Warren and Kincaid were born.

"So are we," affirmed Jeremy. "Now sit down and tell us what you've been up to."

❧

Toni thoroughly enjoyed seeing the twins, who were distinctly different individuals. Their dark hair and eyes reflected their father's Cherokee blood, while their facial features more resembled April's. They were lively but well mannered, making only a mild protest when April told them it was their bedtime.

The twins hugged their father, then held their arms up to Toni, as well.

"You must be very proud of those two," Toni said to Jeremy

after April excused herself to put them to bed and hear their prayers.

"We are. They bless our lives every day."

When April returned, she and Jeremy took turns trying to convince Toni it was time for her to marry a good man and raise a family of her own.

"No, thanks. My life is happy just as it is."

"It could be a lot happier," April said. "It's time you knocked that chip off your shoulder."

"Yes," agreed Jeremy. "Like my grandmother used to say, 'Don't cut off your nose to spite your face.'"

"Or borrow trouble," Toni said. "End of discussion."

However, when April saw Toni to the door, she returned to the subject. "I know you don't want to hear this, but you're missing so much by not giving love a chance."

"You're right—I don't want to hear it. I don't feel I've missed a thing."

Toni spoke confidently, but on her way home, she considered her friends' counsel. April's relative youth hadn't allowed her to become Toni's guardian, but Toni had always looked to her as a role model and valued her advice—at least about most things.

April is wrong about this, though. I'm the best judge of what I should do.

seven

"David just left," Evelyn said when Toni entered the living room shortly before ten o'clock. "He said to tell you he was sorry he didn't get to see you tonight."

"Too bad I can't be in two places at the same time," Toni said lightly.

"Tell me about the Winters. I'd love to see their twin boys again."

Toni and Evelyn chatted for a few minutes before Toni rose and stretched. "I'm going to call it a night. I need to be at church early tomorrow for a final rehearsal."

"David and I will come to the worship service."

Toni felt a tingle of apprehension. A pillar of First Church, Evelyn had allowed Toni to continue attending Community Church with April, but she had visited it only a few times when Toni sang. "Are you sure First Church won't collapse if you don't show up tomorrow?"

"I'm hardly that important," Evelyn said. "Besides, the church will have to do without me soon enough. They might as well get used to it."

ॐ

"We have a full house today," Ted Brown commented when he and Toni entered the sanctuary from the choir room just before eleven o'clock.

"The word must be out that I'm singing," Toni said with a touch of the sarcasm which had been a shield in her teen years.

"Could be," Ted agreed. "Sit on the first pew. I'll hand you the mike when I cue the tape."

"I know the routine," Toni said.

"Just like old times, right?" Ted asked.

Not quite. In those days, there was no David Trent in the congregation.

Toni closed her eyes in silent prayer. *Lord, help me to be calm and sing only to You. Amen.*

When the service began, Toni immersed herself in it, shutting out everything else. She had asked Ted not to introduce her, but when she rose to sing, a murmur of recognition swept through the sanctuary. Toni felt a moment of near panic when she spotted Evelyn and David.

Help me, Lord.

Then, with the first note of "His Eye Is on the Sparrow," everything else dropped away, and Toni sang, as always, to honor her Creator.

Why should I feel discouraged?
Why should the shadows come?
Why should my heart be lonely,
And long for heav'n and home,
When Jesus is my portion,
My constant Friend is He;
His eye is on the sparrow,
And I know He watches me.

I sing because I'm happy,
I sing because I'm free;
For His eye is on the sparrow,
And I know He watches me. . .

After the last triumphant chorus, the final strains of the taped accompaniment died away, followed by a reverent silence. As Toni returned the microphone to Ted, she saw David regarding her intently and wondered what he was thinking.

Not that I care, she tried to tell herself, but the words did not quite ring true.

❧

After the benediction, Evelyn and David stood waiting in

the vestibule for Toni while she made her way up the aisle through a crowd of well-wishers.

"That old hymn is one of my favorites," Evelyn said. "I can't believe how much richer your voice has become in the last few years."

"It's beautiful, and you use it well," David said.

He spoke sincerely, and Toni responded in kind. "The Lord gave it to me. I sing only for His glory."

The music leader joined them in time to hear Toni's testimony. "Mrs. Taylor said it was all she could do to keep from shouting 'Hallelujah!' when she heard you sing, Toni. I'm sure she had plenty of company." He turned to David and held out his hand. "I'm Ted Brown, and you must be David. Toni told me you were visiting your sister."

David shook Ted's hand, looking surprised that Toni had spoken about him. With a final wave, Ted departed, and Toni and David followed Evelyn outside.

"You and David can go in your car," Evelyn directed Toni. "I'll follow in mine."

"Where are we going?" Toni asked Evelyn's retreating back.

"To the DeSoto State Park restaurant," David said. "Do you want me to drive?"

"It's my car," Toni said, less graciously than she intended.

He seemed amused. "So it is."

"I'm used to driving myself, I mean," she added.

"I am too."

Toni winced inwardly. *I'm doing it again. It seems I cannot carry on a simple conversation with this man without sounding like a fool.*

"Why isn't Evelyn riding with us?" Toni asked.

David shrugged. "She said something about wanting to get home early."

Toni said nothing, but she suspected she knew the reason. *Evelyn is trying to get David and me together.*

❧

"It has been years since I've been to the state park," Toni

commented to fill the silence between them as she drove.

"Me too, but when I was a kid, I knew it like the back of my hand. The Scouts used to pitch tents at the campground and hike all the trails. We'd pretend it was the 1540s and we had come from Spain with Hernando DeSoto. We fancied we were the first Europeans to see all the falls and the Little River Canyon."

"I never had a chance to do anything like that," Toni said, aware too late how wistful she had sounded.

"Back then, roughing it was fun."

"These days, people think of that as having to watch a black-and-white television set," Toni said. *How stupid can you get? David must think I'm a dunce at making small talk.*

"Slow down! You're about to miss the turnoff."

David's cry startled Toni, and she applied the brakes so hard the tires squealed. *Take it easy, Buddy. I'm not in the army, and you're not my commander.*

As if he had read her thought, David apologized. "Sorry. I didn't mean to sound like a drill sergeant."

"Then don't talk like one," she said shortly.

To Toni's surprise, David smiled. "Duly noted."

A few moments later, they passed through the entrance gates and Toni parked in the lot near the lodge. Evelyn pulled up beside them almost immediately.

"It must be at least ten degrees cooler up here," David commented as Evelyn joined them.

"That's one reason I like to come up here," she said. "The other is, the food is worth the wait," she added when they saw the large number people lined up for the buffet.

"I hope so," David said. "I had my fill of standing around waiting to be fed in the army."

"I daresay not many mess halls are like this," Evelyn said.

Toni welcomed the ensuing conversation about recent renovations to the lodge and cabins, followed by the food in the buffet in particular and Southern cooking in general. All safe topics.

"That food was definitely great," David said when he finished the last bite of his meringue-topped banana pudding.

"So is the scenery, and you don't have to wait in line for it," Evelyn said. "You and Toni should walk some of the trails."

"What about you?" Toni asked, anticipating the answer.

"I'm going home and take my usual Sunday afternoon nap. Stay here as long as you like. I have nothing planned for the evening."

"Now, that's a switch," David said after Evelyn left. "My sister seems to think I must be kept constantly occupied."

"Same with me. I suppose she wants to be a good hostess."

"Do you really want to go hiking?"

Toni pointed to the two-inch heels on her shoes. "These are hardly made for hiking."

"They'll do for DeSoto Falls. We can park not four hundred feet from it."

Toni hesitated, then handed David the keys to her SUV. "You drive, since you know the way."

David looked as if he might want to say something but took the keys without comment and opened the passenger door for Toni.

Neither spoke during the short drive, but even before David pulled into the parking lot, they heard the distant sound of falling water. "We must be getting close," Toni said.

"You'll soon see."

A constant roar came from the water spilling over the dam, which had been built in 1925 to provide electricity to the Lookout Mountain area.

They watched it for a moment, then started out on the path to the lower falls. It seemed natural when David took Toni's hand on the sometimes rough path and continued to hold it when they stopped at an overlook. They stood quietly, enjoying the view of the huge half circle of rugged cliffs—in shades ranging from brown to rust and white—surrounding the falling water. Below, a seemingly bottomless pool made a circle some 250 feet in diameter. In the fissures of the cliffs, stunted scrub pines and tufts of grass and wildflowers added their colorful accents.

They took in the scene in comfortable silence for some moments. "Awesome, isn't it?" David said over the roar of the water.

Toni nodded. "Every time I see something like this, I think of Psalm 42:7; 'Deep calleth unto deep at the noise of thy water-spouts.' It really shows us a tiny part of God's awesome power."

"You seem to be close to Him."

Toni searched for the right words. "Not as close as I want to be."

"I suppose everyone could say that. There was a time. . ." David broke off speaking and motioned toward a broad rock a few steps away. For awhile they sat in silence and watched the magnificent scene. Rainbows played around the spray as the clear water continually fell in a breathtaking, headlong rush into the pool below them.

"Evelyn is missing a treat," Toni said.

David turned to face her. "I'm glad she didn't stay. I wanted to talk to you alone, for a change."

For a change? You've had many chances, Toni almost said, but checked herself. "What about?"

"I'm leaving tomorrow morning."

Toni looked at him in surprise. "Does Evelyn know?"

He shook his head. "Not yet."

"I'm sure she'll be very disappointed."

"I doubt you will. You don't seem to like me very much."

I didn't want to like you, but I think I do, anyway. "What makes you say that?" Toni asked.

David shrugged. "Your body language, for one. You always seem so skittish. I can tell I make you uneasy, but I don't mean to."

He spoke with such sincerity that Toni felt compelled to reply in kind. "It has nothing to do with you personally."

"Evelyn told me some bad things had happened to you when you were a child. I hope that's all it is."

Toni felt her cheeks warm. "I don't know what she said, but there's no need to feel sorry for me. That was all a long time ago. Besides, I got the impression that you were uncomfortable with me."

He looked surprised. "Not at all. In fact—"

Before she quite realized it was happening, David brought Toni into the circle of his arms and kissed her. Without stopping to think, she returned the brief kiss, then drew back.

Whatever possessed me to do that?

"Oh," she murmured.

David regarded her steadily. "I'll be back soon."

"For another visit?"

"Yes, but I've been talking to some people about buying into a business in Rockdale."

"So you could become more than a visitor." Toni tested the idea. She had thought he would soon be gone. How could she ignore David if he continued to be nearby?

"I hope so." He paused before he spoke again. "When I come back, I'll bring the children."

A thousand waterfalls roared in Toni's head, drowning out all intelligent thought.

"Children?" she repeated. "You have children?"

David looked stricken. "Evelyn didn't tell you?"

Toni shook her head. "No," she said, wondering why. Then the implication hit her. "I suppose these children have a mother?"

David's jaw tightened. "My wife died last year—that's why I left the army."

"I'm so sorry," Toni mumbled, chagrined.

"I suppose I should have mentioned them earlier."

You just forgot to mention them when you were telling me all about your life over a romantic dinner, right? Toni rose and stood, her legs trembling unexpectedly. "Why? You thought I already knew. We'd better leave now."

"Wait," he called, but she had already started toward the path. "I'm sorry for the misunderstanding," he said when he caught up with her.

Misunderstanding?

David looked so contrite that Toni felt inclined to believe him.

"Tell me about your children," she said with as much interest as she could muster.

"Mandy—short for Amanda—is twelve, and Josh is six."

David removed two pictures from his billfold. One showed a smiling blond woman holding an infant; beside her stood an unsmiling little girl.

"That was taken when Josh was just a baby, before Jean got sick."

"Your daughter doesn't look very happy," Toni said.

"Mandy wouldn't smile because she'd lost her front teeth. This one was taken last year."

Toni saw what she took to be the same two children, several years older and photographed against a fake Christmas scene, the girl still unsmiling. "Nice-looking," she said.

David seemed disappointed as he replaced the pictures. "I take it you don't care much for children."

Toni groaned inwardly. *There I go again, saying the wrong thing.* "I wouldn't have lasted very long in social work if I didn't care about kids."

"That's not what I meant," David said.

Toni faced him, her chin high. "Then what did you mean?"

He opened his mouth, then closed it and shrugged. "Nothing. More of the misunderstanding thing, I suppose."

They continued to walk toward the parking lot, but this time David didn't take her hand, and once again Toni wished she knew what he was thinking.

"You can drive home," she said when he offered her the keys.

I know it's a peace offering, David's expression told her, *but I'm not fooled.*

On the drive back, Toni attempted to get David to talk about his family. "It must have been hard on the children when their mother died. Who takes care of them?"

David's mouth formed a straight line. "Jean's mother and stepfather."

"In Virginia?" she guessed.

"Yes, I really thought Evelyn had already told you all of that."

No, but she will.

They drove to Evelyn's house in an awkward silence. David shut off the ignition, handed Toni her keys, and came around to open the passenger door for her.

"Aren't you coming inside?" she asked when he started toward his truck.

"No. Tell Evelyn I'll call later."

It's just as well, Toni thought as she hurried into the house to confront David's sister.

eight

Toni entered the house primed for an immediate showdown. Disappointed to find Evelyn's bedroom door closed, Toni went to the sunroom. As her mind replayed the scene at the falls several times, Toni became increasingly convinced she had every right to be upset.

Evelyn came out of her room a half hour later, obviously surprised to find Toni alone. "Where's David?"

"At the inn, I suppose. He said he'll call you later."

Evelyn looked disappointed. "I expected you two would make an afternoon of it."

"We didn't."

"You look upset. Is something wrong?"

Toni took a deep breath. "Why didn't you tell me about David's children?"

Evelyn's expression reflected genuine surprise. "I've always mentioned David and his family in my Christmas letters. I took it for granted that you knew."

Toni assumed she'd remember if she'd read anything about him, but that didn't mean Evelyn hadn't written it. "I suppose I might have dismissed the family details since I didn't know them," she admitted, making a mental note to be more attentive in the future.

"Even so, it seems the subject would have come up naturally before now."

"David and I talked about our careers, but we never talked about our personal lives, and I gathered he wanted it that way as much as I did. But today when he said he would bring the children with him next time he came, I felt blindsided."

"I'm sorry. You and David seemed to hit it off so well."

"You invited him to Rockdale just to meet me, didn't you?"

Evelyn shook her head. "David has always had a standing invitation, but he was out of the country a lot, then after Jean became ill, he didn't have a chance to go anywhere."

"Didn't you think it odd that David didn't come here when he got out of the army?"

"Not really. His wife had just died, and he had a lot on his mind."

"You're certain you didn't just happen to invite him to come to Rockdale the very week I arrived?"

Evelyn threw up her hands. "You'd make a good prosecuting attorney," she said ruefully. "The only thing I told him was that I planned to retire soon and do some traveling."

"And some matchmaking," Toni added. "Surely you can't deny that."

Evelyn shrugged and shook her head. "Obviously, your mind is made up, but I wish you could accept my brother's presence at this time as a coincidence."

Toni's initial outrage had evaporated, leaving her drained and weary. She attempted a feeble smile. "So that's your story and you're sticking with it."

Evelyn stood. "I have to—it's the truth. I'm going to the inn. I don't suppose you want to come with me?"

Toni could think of nothing she wanted any less at that moment. "No, thanks."

"Is there anything you want me to tell David?"

Tell him it is probably just as well that our brief acquaintance came to an end before it could hurt us both.

Toni didn't know what brought such a thought to her mind, but she would never voice it. She shook her head. "Nothing except good-bye."

Evelyn started out, then stopped to glance back at Toni. "You look tired. Try to get some rest. Things will look different in the morning."

Yes. David will be gone then.

❧

Evelyn had already left when Toni got up Monday morning; a

note on the telephone table said she was at the DHR office.

"I ought to go there too," Toni said aloud. After breakfast, she showered and dressed in a comfortable lemon-lime shift. She had just closed the front door behind her when David's truck pulled up to the curb.

Toni's heart lurched, then began to hammer. She presumed David had already left Rockdale. In any case, she must be the last person he wanted to see.

"Evelyn's at the office," she called from the porch.

David turned off the motor, got out of the truck, and mounted the porch steps. "I know. We said good-bye last night."

Just go away and leave me alone, Toni wanted to say. "I'm on my way to the office myself."

"I won't keep you long. I couldn't leave Rockdale without apologizing for the way I acted yesterday."

Toni attempted to conceal her confusion with a veil of sarcasm. "Is that your idea or Evelyn's?"

"Mine. She said I should have talked to you about the kids from the start, but that's not easy for me. . . ."

David stood so close that Toni could see the pulse in his neck. *He's struggling to say the right thing. It wouldn't kill me to forgive and forget.*

"I can understand that. You don't need to apologize."

"About that kiss—"

"It never happened," Toni said quickly.

David's mouth twisted. "I was kind of hoping it had." For an instant, she thought he was going to kiss her again. Instead, he put out his hand. Almost automatically Toni extended hers, and he pressed it gently. "Good-bye, Miss Toni Schmidt. It was nice meeting you."

He turned to go, and Toni barely resisted the impulse to follow him. "When will you be back?" she called from the safety of the porch.

"I'm not sure. Evelyn can fill you in on my plans. You two take care of yourselves."

"You take care too," she murmured, too low for him to hear.

Toni felt a rush of conflicting emotions as he drove out of sight. Her hope to see David again struggled briefly against the knowledge that she was well rid of him. She had never allowed any man to get close to her, and David Trent should be no different.

That was a vow she still intended to keep.

❧

Evelyn Trent had always seemed to guard her emotions, and she seldom spoke to anyone of personal matters. But that evening when Evelyn brought out the scrapbook containing pictures and mementos of her family, Toni saw how deeply she cared for them. Toni was touched to see several photos of herself among Evelyn's pictures of the Trents.

"What a mess I was in those days," Toni said of a snapshot taken soon after Evelyn had become her guardian.

"You just needed a little cleaning up." Evelyn turned the page. "See how much better you look in your graduation picture."

Toni gazed at the image of herself at eighteen—an unsmiling young woman, her chin slightly raised, ready to take on a world that had been less than kind to her. "At least you made me comb my hair before going out in public."

Evelyn turned to another page. "This is Jean and David when they married in Virginia. She was a civilian employee at the base where he was stationed."

More pictures followed—of Mandy as a baby; as a toddler with an Easter basket; standing beside her mother, who held her baby brother.

"David showed me that picture," Toni said. "Jean must have been quite lovely."

"I never really knew her; she never came to Rockdale."

"Were they overseas when she became ill?" Toni asked.

"Oh, no—Jean went to Germany with David after they married, but she came home to have Mandy and never went back. David was on a four-year stateside tour when Josh was born, then he was sent to Kosovo. Jean became sick while he was there, but he didn't know how ill she was for a long time. Here are the children with their grandmother after the funeral."

"They all look so sad," Toni murmured.

"They were. Even Josh knew something was wrong, but his mother was ill for so long, he scarcely knew her."

Toni picked up a more recent picture of David's daughter. Skinny, straight hair, and unsmiling, she looked uncannily like Toni at that age. "What about Mandy?"

Evelyn sighed. "David is concerned about both children. The Websters—Jean's mother and stepfather—did their best, I suppose, but David left the army to be with his children. He wants to put down roots and make them feel like a real family again."

"When do you think that will happen?"

Evelyn closed the album and leaned back in her chair. "David has business to take care of in Virginia, but he asked me to find something he can rent here."

"What about this house? It would make more sense for me to rent an apartment and let them live here."

Evelyn smiled faintly. "I offered to let them live here with me after Jean's death and again the other day, but he turned me down again. He thinks this house—where we grew up—is too small." She sighed as if resigning herself to never understand her brother's reasoning.

"I'll gladly move if he changes his mind." Toni spoke sincerely. "I hope things will work out for them."

Evelyn sighed. "So do I. They all deserve better than what they've had."

❧

For the next two weeks, Toni stayed so busy learning the DHR routines and procedures she had little time to think of anything else. Soon Evelyn would be gone, and while Toni knew she could never replace her, she wanted the transition to be as smooth as possible. She felt pleasantly surprised when some of the people who had once called her JD, short for juvenile delinquent, now went out of their way to make her feel welcome. She also enjoyed her renewed friendship with Mary Oliver.

"It's so good to have someone I can talk to," Mary told Toni over a salad at Statum's one evening.

"From the reception you got at the reunion, I'd say you have a whole bunch of friends."

"I teach some of their children—that could have something to do with it. They like me in that role, but I know some of them also feel sorry for me. They think my life will be a big zero unless I get married."

"And you disagree, of course," said Toni.

Mary paused her fork in midair and leaned forward. "I wouldn't say this to just anyone, but I think you'll understand. I believe God called me to be a teacher and has let me remain single so I can give all my love to my first-graders—especially the ones who don't get much attention at home."

"I believe I was called to do social work too," Toni said, "but that has nothing to do with my decision not to marry."

Mary was silent for a moment, as if recalling what she knew about Toni's background. "You haven't gotten over what happened to your mother, have you?"

"How could I? Believe me, her mistakes taught me lessons about men and marriage I can never forget."

"Maybe you should try to let go of your bitterness," Mary suggested.

"I'm not bitter," Toni insisted. "I just don't intend to get married."

"Not even if the right man comes along?"

"That hasn't happened."

Mary smiled. "At least not yet."

"Not ever. Case closed."

They went on to talk about other things, but that night Toni pondered what Mary words. Toni had never thought of her feelings about marriage in that way, but even if it were true, didn't she have every right to be bitter?

Maybe you should pray about it.

Although she had not voiced the words, Toni shook her head violently.

"There's nothing to pray about," she said aloud, but without a great deal of confidence.

Her confusion was all David Trent's fault. He would soon be back in Rockdale, but after Evelyn left town, he would be easier to avoid—and her life would be much simpler.

nine

Toni expected David Trent would surely return to Rockdale to attend his sister's retirement dinner. However, he still hadn't arrived by the time Evelyn and Toni left for the country club that Friday night.

Evelyn thought only Toni and her fellow workers would be there; she did not know her "small dinner" would turn out to be held in a ballroom packed with well-wishers. Judge Oliver, who served as the master of ceremonies, ushered an astounded Evelyn to the dais, where Congressman Winter, Police Chief Hurley, and Mayor Hastings were already seated. After dinner, each delivered a short speech expressing their own and Rockdale's appreciation for Evelyn's years of service. Finally, President Newman Howell of Rockdale Bank brought in a set of luggage, which he presented Evelyn along with tickets for a Caribbean cruise.

"We wanted to help you get started on all that retirement travel you've talked about for so long."

Obviously moved, Evelyn could not immediately speak. "Of course I thank you all, but I suspect you people really want me to get out of town."

Toni joined in the standing ovation that followed, touched by the obvious affection the town Evelyn Trent had served so long now bestowed upon her.

David should be here to see this. Toni had supplied Judge Oliver with David's telephone number, so he must have been invited. She felt a moment of uneasiness that something might have happened to him, then Evelyn spoke again.

"Thank you, thank you—please sit down. And now, there's someone here I want to make sure you all get to know."

Evelyn gestured to Toni, and again the crowd applauded.

Toni felt the blood rush to her face as she made her way to the dais to stand beside Evelyn. She had refused Judge Oliver's earlier suggestion that she sit there, telling him the evening was Evelyn's and she alone deserved attention.

"This is Toni Schmidt, my most able replacement. I trust you will give her the same support that you always gave me."

More applause followed, along with a few scattered cries of "Speech!"

"Say something," Evelyn urged. She propelled Toni to the microphone and grasped her arm as if to make sure she stayed there.

When the applause died down, Toni looked at Evelyn, then at the audience. "I join you all in wishing Evelyn Trent a happy retirement, but let me correct one thing she said. I may sit in the same office behind the same desk, but I think we all know that no one could ever replace this great lady."

"Well said," Judge Oliver declared to more applause. "Thank you all for coming." He turned from the microphone and spoke to Evelyn. "Stand by the door and let everyone greet you on their way out."

Evelyn held Toni by the arm. "Stay with me. I want to make sure you meet everyone."

Toni had no choice but to do as Evelyn directed. By the time the last person had filed by, Toni's hand ached from being enthusiastically shaken.

"I don't know how you politicians do it," she told Jeremy Winter, who had lingered to talk to Judge Oliver. "I've smiled so much my face is about to crack open, and my hand's ready to drop off."

Jeremy chuckled. "I'll share our secrets with you sometime."

"How long will you and April be here?"

"We head back to Washington next week."

"Tell April to call me—maybe we can get together after church."

"Will do." He turned to Evelyn. "In case April and I don't see you again before we leave, know that we wish you the best."

"So do we all," echoed Margaret Hastings, bringing up the rear.

❧

"This evening has been a bit overwhelming," Evelyn admitted to Toni on the way home. "You knew they were going to do that to me, didn't you?" Without waiting for her confirmation, she went on. "I wish someone had told David this dinner would be such a grand affair. He should have been there."

Toni opened her mouth to say that David knew, then stopped, unwilling to get into something that was none of her business. *David Trent can make his own excuses.*

"The mayor's assistant videotaped the speeches, so he can see what happened," Toni said. "That's something else you didn't expect."

Evelyn sighed. "I never dreamed anyone would want to make such a fuss over me."

"You deserve every bit of it. You've always done much more than you were paid to do," Toni said.

Evelyn drove her sedan into the garage, shut off the motor, and turned to Toni. "You'll do a good job too, and someday, God willing, you'll have your own retirement dinner. I just pray that long before then you'll also have a good husband to share it with. That's about the only thing that could have made this night better for me."

Toni was surprised that Evelyn still felt so much sorrow that she had remained single. She considered saying so, but Evelyn left the car before Toni had the chance.

It's just as well. Evelyn doesn't understand how I feel about marriage and probably never will. That's one subject better left alone.

❧

David Trent returned to Rockdale on the Friday of Toni's first full week in his sister's former position. She discovered he was back over lunch at Statum's when she heard Nelson Neal, the manager of Rockdale's only condominium complex, tell Tom Statum that he'd finally rented his last vacant unit.

"Evelyn Trent paid the deposit last week and the tenants showed up this morning—a man and two kids. I believe the fellow's Ms. Trent's brother."

Tom nodded. "Yes, David Trent's been here several times lately. I didn't know he had kids."

Toni smiled inwardly. *That makes two of us, Tom.*

"Yep, a girl about twelve and a boy who looks about five. Didn't either of them seem real happy about moving here."

"Carryout up," a waitress called from the kitchen, and the condo manager took his food and left without further conversation.

Toni's mind whirled. Evelyn hadn't said anything more about when David would return—in fact, they hadn't spoken of him at all since the night of the retirement dinner, and Toni suspected it was deliberate. That morning, Evelyn had said she might not be back by the time Toni got home from work; she had several things to see to before leaving on her cruise next week. Toni wondered whether David might be the cause of at least one of those errands.

Evelyn had walked to work in all but the worst weather, and Toni planned to do the same. On her way home that evening, she thought of the first time she'd seen David Trent, waiting on the front porch—for her or for Evelyn, she never knew which. Was it possible that David would be there now?

It's not likely. He and the children will have had a long day, and he probably already knows Evelyn isn't there. He has no reason to go to her house.

Toni had so convinced herself that he wouldn't be there that she felt a jolt of surprise when turned down Maple Street and spotted David's truck parked in front of the house. Then she saw David sitting in the front porch swing just as he had the day they met. The man was every bit as handsome as she remembered, but when he stood to greet her, he seemed unusually grave.

"Where are the children?" Toni asked.

"In the yard out back. How did you know they were with

me? Not even Evelyn knew exactly when we were coming."

"The famous Rockdale grapevine," Toni said.

David pointed to Toni's briefcase. "I see you're already hard at work."

"Yes, last Friday was Evelyn's last day. I'm on my own now."

Had David's eyes always been so blue? Toni swallowed hard and tried to concentrate. "Rockdale gave your sister a wonderful retirement dinner. She was disappointed that you missed it."

"The judge called me with a heads up, but I couldn't have gotten everything packed for the move that soon. Besides, it was Evelyn's night to shine. I would have been in the way."

"So you're here to stay now?"

"If you could see all the stuff I unloaded today, you wouldn't have to ask. Even without furniture, I managed to fill a pretty good-sized moving trailer with our stuff."

"I suppose you know Evelyn's not home."

"Yes, but I hoped you could join us for pizza tonight."

I want you to meet my children, and I don't quite know how to go about doing it, Toni read in David's expression.

She hesitated. Her mind urged her to say no now and keep on declining David's invitations until he finally got the message—she wanted nothing to do with him or his children. However, her heart, which had betrayed her by beating faster the moment she saw him, spoke for her instead.

"All right." Toni glanced at her dry-clean-only business suit. "I'd better change first."

David relaxed visibly. "Sure, take your time. I'll round up the kids."

From inside the house, Toni heard David calling and the children's voices answering, but she couldn't make out any words. She exchanged her office outfit for blue jeans and a white shirt and started back to the front porch. Hearing the children's voices through the screen door, Toni stopped to listen. David stood with his back to her, blocking her view of the swing where the children sat.

"I'm huuungry," the little boy whined.

"I'm starved," the older girl complained. "How much longer do we have to wait before we can eat?"

Taking the cue, Toni opened the screen door and stepped onto the porch. "Not much longer," she said.

David looked relieved. "That didn't take long." He stepped aside and pointed out the children with the flourish of a painter unveiling a portrait. "You've seen their pictures, now here they are in the flesh—Joshua David and Amanda Jean Trent. Kids, this is Miss Toni Schmidt."

The boy scowled. "Daddy, you know my name's Josh."

"And I'm really Mandy," the girl corrected.

Toni nodded and shook their hands in turn. "You may call me Toni."

David gave them a weak smile. "Seems I didn't get anyone's name right, but now that the introductions are over, who wants pizza?"

"Me!" Josh jumped out of the swing and ran down the steps, followed closely by his shrieking sister, each determined to get to the truck first.

"They're not always this loud," David said apologetically. "It's been a long day, and they're used to having supper an hour earlier in Virginia."

"They obviously have good lungs." *That was a stupid thing to say. Why do I always say idiotic things around David Trent?*

David walked beside Toni to the truck and opened the passenger door. "While you were changing, I used my cell phone to order a couple of pizzas with the works. I hope that's acceptable."

I'm not fond of pizza, I don't usually eat supper this early, and if those kids keep up their carrying on, I'm sure to have a fine case of indigestion. Toni's better nature told her to be civil.

"Yes, that's fine. I'm not a big pizza eater, though. Maybe you'll have enough left for another meal."

"Not with Josh around," Mandy said.

"You eat lots more 'n I do," her brother protested.

"Don't either!"

"Do so!"

"That's enough," David said sternly.

Except for some furtive pinching and poking between them, Josh and Mandy behaved during the rest of the drive to the pizza restaurant.

"Did you used to come here when you were a kid, Daddy?" Josh asked when they had been seated.

"Pizza probably wasn't even invented that long ago," said Mandy.

"Actually, I think pizza goes back quite a few centuries," Toni said, then wanted to bite her tongue. *I sound like a prissy schoolmarm.* It appeared that the trouble she had talking to David also applied to his children.

Fortunately, the pizzas arrived soon after they were seated, and the children devoted their full attention to eating. Toni noticed their table manners could use a little work, but she didn't call it to David's attention. They were his children; teaching them the rudiments of etiquette wasn't her job.

"You'll have to come by and see the condo," David invited. "It's no palace, but it's within walking distance of both their schools, and that's a plus."

"That's right, school will be starting soon, won't it?" Toni recalled Mary Oliver's recent complaint that summers seemed to get shorter every year.

Mandy made a face. "I don't want to go to school in this dinky town."

"Dinky, stinky!" Josh sang out until silenced by David's glare.

Toni tried again. "Rockdale may be a small town, but the schools are excellent."

Mandy rolled her eyes at Toni's pronouncement. "Not as good as my school back home in Virginia. All my friends are there."

"Virginia isn't our home anymore," David said gently.

"That's what you say. I don't care where you make me and Josh live, we'll always want to go back to Virginia."

Seeing that Mandy was on the verge of tears, Josh apparently decided to cry too. "Home! I wanna go home!"

"People are looking at us," David said. "You know how to act better than that."

In spite of herself, Toni felt sorry for David. *He seems to want to be a good father, but he doesn't know how.*

"Go wash your face," David told Mandy when the last of the pizza had been eaten. "It's wall-to-wall pizza."

"Josh has more on his mouth than I have on my whole face," Mandy said.

"Do not!"

"I'll tend to your brother," David said pointedly, and Mandy flounced off in a huff. "Come on, Son, let's repair the damage."

"I don't wanna have my face washed!"

David lifted Josh from his chair, set him on his feet, and hugged him against his hip, minimizing any arm-flailing as they headed toward the rest room. The boy squealed loudly and attracted a lot of attention.

Some of the diners looked at Toni as if to say that she was a rotten mother, David was a rotten father, and their children were just plain rotten.

Spoiled rotten. It didn't take a child psychologist to figure out how David's children had gotten that way. Their father had been absent much of the time, and Toni guessed their mother hadn't been a disciplinarian even before she became ill. After they went to live with their grandparents, they were probably allowed to do pretty much what they wanted. To get back on the right path, they needed a loving but firm father—and someone to be a mother figure.

Their aunt was the ideal candidate, but Evelyn probably wouldn't be around them enough to have much influence.

I guess that conveniently leaves just you, doesn't it? Toni's pesky inner voice inquired.

"Be quiet," she told it, and for the moment, it obeyed.

Mandy returned with a clean face and a more subdued

manner, and Toni stood. "My face probably needs attention too. I'll be right back."

"I think we're ready to call it a night," David said when Toni rejoined them.

The children had talked earlier of going for ice cream after the pizza, but fatigue had erased it from their minds. Mandy managed to walk to the truck under her own power, but David had to carry Josh, who was already half asleep.

Toni felt strangely moved by the quiet child in David's arms. *Josh looks like a little angel. It's too bad he won't stay that way.*

Both children were sleeping when David reached Evelyn's house. Lights inside confirmed she was there, but Toni correctly surmised that David wouldn't go inside.

"Tell Evelyn we'll see her tomorrow."

Toni grasped the door handle. "Thanks for the pizza."

"Wait."

David came around to the passenger side and helped Toni out. Aware of every detail—the scent of his aftershave, the warmth of his hand on hers, the fact that he stood so very close—Toni felt oddly breathless.

It couldn't have been more than a few seconds, but it seemed ages to her before David spoke. "Thanks for putting up with the kids. I'm afraid they weren't at their best tonight."

Toni ignored the strange fluttering in her chest and adopted her best social worker tone. "I understood that they were tired and stressed. Moving to a new place is never easy."

David's intense gaze suggested that he saw through her attempt at detachment. "Do you think there's any hope for us?"

Toni felt a thrill of alarm. Which *us* is he talking about? But it made no difference, since she would not be a part of David Trent's "us."

Toni raised her chin and spoke firmly. "You and the children will do just fine. Good night, David."

And we will be quite fine without each other, as well, Mr. Trent.

Trying to believe it, Toni turned and went into the house.

ten

As Toni suspected she would do, Evelyn headed for her brother's condominium early Saturday morning.

"He'll need some help getting things straight."

Relieved that Evelyn hadn't urged Toni to go with her, she volunteered to bring their lunch.

"Thanks. Come around noon. David's is the first ground floor unit on the left."

Toni hurried through her usual Saturday chores, then called Tom Statum and ordered sandwiches and fixings for three adults and two children.

After she showered, Toni put on a cotton shift and filled a cooler with cold sodas. She put paper plates and napkins and disposable utensils in a plastic bag in case they were needed.

"You must be headed to David Trent's condo," Tom said when he handed Toni her order. "I put in a little something extra for the kids," he added.

Toni didn't want Tom to think she and David Trent were spending time together. "Thanks. Evelyn has been over there all morning—I'm delivering their lunch."

"Tell David I'm glad he decided to come back home," Tom said.

Even without Evelyn's directions, Toni would have had no trouble finding David's condo. His truck stood alone in the first parking spot on the left, and a rental trailer partially blocked the sidewalk in front of the corresponding unit.

"Daddy, she's here!"

Josh had apparently been kneeling on the couch, watching for her from the front window. When Toni came in, he threw both arms around her legs, almost tripping her. "What you got? I'm hungry."

73

"Lunch, but the drinks and plates are still in the back of my SUV."

David came from the adjacent kitchen and took the sack from Toni. Even in his ragged cutoff jeans and a sweat-stained, olive drab T-shirt, David still looked attractive.

"Thanks. Did you say there's more to bring in?"

"Yes. Mandy, would you like to help me?"

"I guess so," she said without enthusiasm.

"I'll do it!" Josh exclaimed. "Let me, let me!"

"She didn't ask you, Dummy—all you do is drop things," Mandy said.

"Josh can help too," Toni said quickly.

Mandy muttered under her breath. "Sure, whiny baby always gets his way."

Pretending she hadn't heard, Toni led the way to her SUV and handed Mandy the cooler.

Josh danced up and down. "My turn, my turn," he sang.

Toni tied the handles of the plastic bag together so he could carry it more easily. "These are the paper plates and napkins. We can't eat without them."

Mandy left with the cooler, but Josh stayed and watched Toni close the rear hatch. For the first time she noticed how blue the boy's eyes were. Just like his father's. *Josh is going to be a handsome young man.*

The boy obviously wanted to say something but seemed to be having a hard time getting it out. "What is it?" Toni prompted.

"Are you our new mommy?"

Toni felt her jaw slacken in shock. *Did Josh really say what I thought I heard?*

"What makes you ask that?"

"Daddy said we'd get a new mommy when we came here."

"When did he tell you that?"

Josh shrugged and shifted the bag to his other hand. "I dunno—a long time ago."

Not knowing how to answer, Toni asked him a question. "Do you want a new mommy?"

Josh's blue eyes filled with tears. "I want my old mommy to come back from heaven. I want to go back home to Nana Alice."

Lord, show me what to say to this child.

Toni put her hand on his shoulder and spoke earnestly. "I know how much you must miss your mommy, but heaven is a wonderful place and I'm sure your mommy is happy there. I know you miss your grandma too, but we don't always get everything we want, Josh. Things work out if we wait and have patience first."

Josh wiped his eyes with the back of his hand and wrinkled his nose. "I don't like to wait."

"I know you don't, and neither do I. You know what? I'm ready to eat. How about you?"

His face brightened. "Me too!"

Josh ran ahead of Toni and handed the bag to Evelyn, who stood in the doorway. "I was on my way to see what was keeping you. We're all about worked out." Like David, Evelyn looked hot and tired.

"So I see." Toni moved a couple of boxes from the kitchen table and dealt out paper plates and cold soda. "I'm not sure what Tom sent, David, but he said to tell you he's glad to have you back in town."

"I suspect he'll get a lot of our business," David said. "Cooking isn't my favorite thing."

Evelyn piled the wrapped sandwiches and packaged chips in the middle of the table. "There's enough here to feed a small army."

The children needed no invitation to come to the table. Mandy was in the act of unwrapping a sandwich when Evelyn stopped her. "Maybe you haven't been doing it where you lived before, but here we thank God for our food before we eat. Don't we, David?"

David looked surprised, but he nodded and bowed his head. The children followed suit, although Josh watched his father intently.

"Thank You for bringing us here safely, Lord. Thank You for this food and all our other blessings. In Jesus' name, amen."

Not bad, Evelyn's glance suggested.

Toni sighed and wished that Evelyn wasn't going away. She'd have her brother and his family under control in no time, just as she had once straightened out Toni.

"Did you and Josh go to church in Virginia?" Evelyn asked Mandy.

The question produced a moderate amount of eye rolling. "Sometimes Nana Alice took us, but mostly she didn't," Mandy said. "Larry never went."

"Larry?" asked Evelyn.

"That's what Jean's stepfather wanted to be called," said David.

"Larry says there's too many hippos in church," Josh explained.

Toni tried not to smile. She'd heard it said that churches were filled with hypocrites, but she'd never heard them called "hippos" before.

Mandy was quick with an ungracious correction. "Hippos are big, ugly animals. Hypocrites are people who pretend to be good but aren't. You don't know what you're talking about."

Evelyn spoke before the argument could escalate. "You should take the children to Sunday school tomorrow, David."

Josh made a growling sound. "Ugh, school! I hate school!"

"You don't know anything about school, Dummy. I've told you before, kindergarten isn't real school."

"It is so too!" Josh said.

"Be quiet, both of you," Evelyn said. "Mandy, don't ever call anyone 'dummy' again. Your brother is every bit as smart as you are, and calling other people names only makes you look bad."

Mandy sighed loudly. "He's always saying dumb stuff, though."

David finally found his voice. "You're the big sister and should know better. You should help Josh, not put him down."

Evelyn's sudden laughter startled them all. "Oh, David, you

sounded so much like Dad just then. He was always reminding me what an obligation a big sister had to her little brother."

Josh's eyes grew large. "You're my daddy's big sister?"

Evelyn nodded. "Yes, just like you and Mandy."

Josh looked puzzled. "I thought you were my daddy's mommy."

For a moment, Evelyn looked as if she didn't know whether to laugh or cry, then she rose from the table and laid her hand on Josh's shoulder. "I saw something in the bottom of the lunch sack I think you might like."

Tom's brownies were a big hit, and the children seemed almost calm after eating. They helped clear away the trash without complaint and even followed Evelyn's suggestion to go to their rooms to rest.

"I wish you could stick around longer," David told Evelyn, echoing Toni's sentiments. "You're so good with the kids."

Evelyn spoke with some asperity. "I'm an old maid who never had any children of my own. Everyone knows we don't know beans about raising children."

"They can't say that about you." David gestured toward Toni. "There's living proof that you know how it's done."

As she always did when a conversation turned personal, Toni felt uncomfortable. *Leave me out of this, please.*

Evelyn seemed to answer Toni's mute entreaty. "We're talking about your children, not Toni. They've been through a hard time, and they'll need all the help they can get. Start by taking them to Sunday school. They can meet some children before school starts, and making friends in a new place is important."

"I'll think about it," David said. "We should get back to work now."

"Leave me out of that 'we,'" Evelyn said. "I have some things to do at home. Maybe Toni will stay awhile."

Here we go again. Will her matchmaking never cease?

Yet, in all fairness, Toni knew Evelyn hadn't started packing for her cruise, and time was growing short. Still, intentional or not, it created another chance for Toni and David to be together.

"Don't feel you have to stay," David said quickly.

I think I want to. The admission surprised Toni, and she adopted a tone of indifference. "I suppose I could help for a little while."

Evelyn looked smug. "Good-bye, you two. Want to meet somewhere to eat tonight?"

"I don't think the kids and I are up to another dinner out just yet," David said. "Maybe tomorrow?"

"Toni arranged for us to meet the Winters at DeSoto State Park after church. You and the children can join us."

Anywhere but there, Toni half expected David to say, but he nodded. "Sure—the kids will enjoy seeing the waterfalls."

"We can ride together—but try to take the children to Sunday school first."

David smiled. "Yes, Granny."

"You're lucky I don't have anything to throw at you, Sonny," Evelyn grumbled.

"You don't really look old enough to be David's mother," Toni assured her.

"Tell Josh that. I'll see you at supper, Toni."

"I won't be here that long," Toni called after her.

"I realize you have much better things to do on a Saturday afternoon, but it would really help to get the kitchen things put away," David said.

David told her that Evelyn had unpacked and washed the dishes and glasses and left them on the counter near the cabinets where she thought they should logically be stored.

"I can reach the top shelf, so if you can hand me the things, I'll put them away," David suggested.

It appeared to be safe enough, but Toni soon found the task perilous. Their hands inevitably brushed, and Toni couldn't deny the pleasant sensation of David's touch.

Does he feel it too?

Toni glanced at David, but he seemed totally absorbed in

the orderly, almost military, placement of each item. They moved from cabinet to cabinet, working together in a smooth rhythm, until the counters were empty.

"That takes care of that job," Toni said. "Anything else you need me to do?"

"Nothing, thanks."

This would be a good time to tell David what Josh said to me about getting a new mommy, Toni's inner voice suggested, but she quickly dismissed it. That was a subject best left alone, particularly given Josh's tendency to get things wrong.

Toni gathered her keys and purse. At the door, she turned and spoke again. "Will you be taking the children to First?"

David's jaw tightened almost imperceptibly. "Their things haven't been unpacked, and I don't know where their good clothes are. Tell Evelyn we probably won't make it."

"But you will meet us at the park?"

David gazed at her intently. "Yes, I'll be at the park—again."

Maybe things will work out better this time, his expression said.

Don't count on it, thought Toni.

"Good-bye, then."

Toni was aware that David stood at the door and watched her leave; once again, she wished she knew what he was thinking.

❧

Toni ran a few errands and came home to find Evelyn in the sunroom, reading the newspaper.

"I've packed everything I can for now, and it's too hot to sit on the porch," she said before Toni could ask.

"Air conditioning is a blessing on a day like this," Toni said. "This must be the warmest day we've had since I got back."

"Another good reason to go to DeSoto tomorrow." Evelyn paused, and Toni sensed the subject was about to change, probably for the worse. "Now that you've met them, what do you think of David's children?"

For starters, they are spoiled brats, Toni could have said, except it would not be a fair assessment. In any case, she was reluctant to criticize them to their aunt.

Toni chose her words with care. "I haven't been around them much. They're livelier than they looked in their pictures. Both are attractive and intelligent—and obviously something of a challenge. I'm sorry you won't be around to help David with them."

"My brother knew I'd be going away for long periods of time. Besides, I made it clear I had no intention of raising his children."

"They're going to need someone's help."

Evelyn sighed. "I had hoped. . . ," she began, then stopped. "That's one reason the children should become involved in church activities. Having good teachers during the school week and moral instruction in Sunday school will go a long way to get those two on the right track."

"David said not to expect them at church tomorrow. He said they hadn't unpacked their clothes yet, but I also got the feeling that he doesn't really want to go himself."

"I think you're right. David grew up going to church, but after he went into the army, he drifted away. He won't talk about it, but I suspect Jean's illness and death tested his faith severely."

"I had already guessed as much," said Toni. "I'm surprised that you got him to come to Community Church."

Evelyn smiled. "That wasn't my doing—he wanted to hear you sing."

"He went to be polite."

"There are none so blind as those who will not see," Evelyn quoted the adage. "I've noticed the way David looks at you, Toni. He needs you—and his children need you."

His children need a mother, you mean. And I seem to have been nominated and elected without ever knowing I was on the ballot.

Toni determined to end a conversation that had become increasingly uncomfortable. "What I need is the freedom to do the best possible job I can at the Rockdale DHR office. That's the only work I came here to do."

"Maybe so, but if the Lord intends something more for

you, don't stubbornly close the door to His will."

Evelyn's words were a heartfelt expression of her unspoken affection, and Toni accepted them in the same way.

"If I see God's purpose at work, I'll do it," she promised, and Evelyn seemed satisfied.

Long after they had gone on to other topics, Evelyn's advice stayed in Toni's mind. She had felt God's leadership in her choice of social work and again when she made the decision to come to Rockdale.

Could God have something else in store for me now?

And if so, would she be willing to accept it?

eleven

It was one thing to agree that Toni and Evelyn, the Winters, and David and his children would all meet at DeSoto Park for lunch on Sunday; working out the logistics was another matter.

Since the Winters would be at Community Church, Toni left her SUV parked there and rode to the park with them and the twins. David was to pick up Evelyn when she got home from the service at First.

The morning had been hot and muggy, and by the time the Trents arrived at the park, thunderheads had begun to build in the western sky.

"I don't like the looks of those clouds," Toni heard Evelyn say to David as they approached the verandah where she sat with Jeremy and April. Josh spotted the twins playing under a huge oak tree nearby, and Mandy nearly stumbled over him when he stopped to stare.

"A summer storm could blow in later. Maybe it'll clear the air down in the valley," David answered Evelyn.

"Jeremy, I don't think you've met my brother, David," Evelyn said.

The congressman extended his hand. "No, but Toni's been telling us about you."

David shook Jeremy's hand, then glanced at Toni as if speculating about what she had said.

"This is my wife, April," Jeremy added.

"Hi, David. Toni and I have been friends for ages."

Evelyn called to Josh and Mandy, who were looking at the acorns the twins had gathered. "Come here, kids."

All four scrambled onto the verandah, and Toni made the introductions.

82

"Warren and Kincaid, meet Josh and Mandy."

The twins, sons of a politician, were accustomed to meeting people and solemnly shook hands all around. Josh had never met any twins; he was fascinated that the boys looked so much alike and also had the same birthday.

Evelyn herded the children toward the dining room. "You'll have more time to play after lunch. Let's go inside before the buffet line gets any longer."

Jeremy and April's entrance into the dining room initiated a ripple of conversation as first one person, then another, recognized them. Some diners waved in greeting, while others came up to speak to their congressman. Several older women fussed over the boys, embarrassing them and slowing the family's progress through the line.

"Is it always like this when you go out?" David asked when the Winters finally joined the others at a large table in the rear of the dining room.

"No, sometimes it's worse," April replied. "It's altogether different in Washington. No one pays us any attention."

"There's lots of kids to play with there," added Warren, the more outgoing twin.

"There aren't many children in our Rockdale neighborhood," Jeremy said.

"The next time you're here, our boys should get together," said David. "Josh is just about their age."

"I'm the oldest," Kincaid declared.

"I'm the smartest," Warren boasted.

"I'm gonna be in first grade," said Josh, not to be outdone.

Toni smiled at the children's banter, then noticed David regarding her with the intense expression she'd seen before. Embarrassed, she turned her attention to her plate, listening to but not entering the eddy of conversation swirling around her.

Jeremy leaned across the table and said, "David, Toni says you're back in Rockdale to stay. What are you going to do?"

"It's still up in the air, but when the children are settled in school, I expect to close a deal on a business."

Toni tried to pretend she hadn't heard and wasn't interested. *What David Trent does is his business and none of mine.*

"I've always believed the small businessman is the backbone of the American economy. If my office can help you in any way, just let me know," Jeremy said.

"I knew David needed to meet you," Evelyn said. "He hasn't told me exactly what he's up to, but I'm glad he's come home."

"So glad that she's leaving town," David countered.

"I heard about the cruise you were given," April told Evelyn. "Congratulations—you deserve a happy retirement."

Evelyn smiled ruefully. "You didn't feel that kindly toward me when I wouldn't let you become Toni's guardian."

"You're not going to hold my inexperience against me, are you?" April teased.

David looked puzzled, so Jeremy explained. "Maybe you didn't know that your sister thought April wasn't mature enough to take charge of someone only a few years younger."

"Toni was already my friend, and I wanted to help her," April added. "But Evelyn was right, as always."

Toni spoke with an edge of irritation. "I wish you all wouldn't discuss me as if I'm not even here."

The children had been talking among themselves, but Mandy raised her head at Toni's remark and looked at her with a spark of recognition.

That's exactly the way people treat me, her expression seemed to say.

"Sorry," April said. "All of that was a long time ago, anyway." She looked around the table. "It seems we've all finished eating. I wonder if anyone here would like to see a waterfall."

Immediately, all three boys jumped from their chairs, waving their hands in the air and calling out "Me!" "Me!" and "I do!"

"I wish I had half their energy," Evelyn said. "If you don't mind, I'll do my communing with Nature from the verandah."

The sun was still shining, but the western sky had darkened ominously by the time they left the lodge. Evelyn chose a rocker near the lodge entrance. "If you hear thunder, grab the kids and run. You don't want to get caught in a lightning storm up here," she told David.

"That's for sure. We'll go to the Lodge Falls—it's not far."

Jeremy and April started down the path, with the children running back and forth ahead and around them like a pack of playful puppies.

"It must be hard to have a happy marriage and raise a family under the pressures of Jeremy's job, but they seem to be succeeding," Evelyn remarked.

April turned out to be a stronger person than anyone gave her credit for, Toni might have said if David hadn't been there.

"I'm thankful for good men who are willing to take up politics, but that isn't for me," said David.

"What is? When are you going to tell us about the business you mentioned to Jeremy?" asked Evelyn.

David shrugged. "Nothing has been settled, so it would be premature to say anything yet. But don't worry, you and Toni will be the first to know."

Don't include me—your plans are not my concern.

"I hope so," said Evelyn. "I don't want to have to hear it from Tom Statum."

"You won't." David turned to Toni. "We should go on now. The others will wonder what happened to us."

"Won't you come along?" Toni asked Evelyn. "It's an easy path."

"No, thanks. I'm right where I want to be. I'm practicing for my cruise."

And three's a crowd? Toni wondered.

"I suppose I should catch up and help keep my kids in line," David said soon after they started on the path.

"April and Jeremy can handle them. Have you noticed how well they've behaved around the twins?"

"You mean compared to the bratty way they usually act?"

Toni felt her face redden and regretted speaking at all. "All children need to be with others their own age. They'll be happier when school starts."

David dug his hands into his jeans pockets and sighed. "I

hope you're right. In the meantime, maybe you could show us some of the bike trails where you and April used to ride."

Toni felt a prick of alarm. David seemed to know so much about her, compared to what she knew about him.

"I suppose Evelyn told you about that."

"She mentioned you liked bicycling. I thought it was something I could do with Mandy and Josh that would also be good exercise."

"I'm afraid I'm pretty rusty. I didn't have the time to ride much when I lived in Atlanta."

"Then it's time you got started again," he said.

In the gloom of the level forest through which they walked, they saw Mandy in the far distance but could barely hear her faint call. "Hey, you slowpokes! Hurry up! Come on!"

When David raised his hand, signaling she had been heard, Mandy turned back and went on. "I suppose Mandy thinks the falls will stop running if we don't get there in the next five minutes."

"Could be she's right."

Unaccountably, a vestige of the old, "wild," Toni surfaced. "Want to race?" she asked, already running before David had a chance to answer her challenge.

The path led through a forest floor carpeted with last year's leaves and strewn with acorns, pine cones, and small limbs. The flat-heeled shoes that had served her well on pavement skidded on the path's surface and offered Toni no traction. She rapidly lost ground to David, whose hiking boots were far more suited for the terrain. Aware he was close behind, Toni redoubled her efforts. She saw Mandy just ahead, standing to one side of the trail. As Toni ran past, Mandy stared at her as if she had suddenly gone stark, raving mad.

Mandy might not be far off the mark, she thought.

Toni scarcely had time to consider that possibility before another concern took its place. She was aware of a distant flash of light, followed by a low, rumbling sound that seemed to begin in the bowels of nearby Little River Canyon and rise, amplified by the beating of her heart, to fill her head.

Toni tried to stop, but the path suddenly tilted downhill, and she had built up so much momentum she had to keep running. Panting from the unaccustomed exertion, Toni had almost managed to brake her headlong rush when she stumbled. As if in slow motion, she saw the ground rushing up to meet her and closed her eyes, bracing for the inevitable impact.

Instead, she felt David's arms encircle her, drawing her close to him. They hit the ground, with David's body absorbing most of the shock.

He spoke roughly. "Are you trying to break every bone in your body?" He breathed hard, and when she raised her head, Toni saw on his face a mixture of anger and some other emotion she could not read.

She struggled in his grip, trying to sit up. "It seems you're doing that for me quite nicely."

His grasp loosened and he sat back. "I'm sorry if I hurt you, but if I hadn't stopped you—"

April ran up to them, concern evident on her face and in her voice. "Are you all right?"

"Of course I am." Toni looked at David, who was still recovering his breath. "I was just winning a race."

"It looked more like you were playing football," April said.

Jeremy reached them, trailed by the children. All were out of breath from running.

"I hope you have enough wind left to get back to the lodge," Jeremy said. "That thunder sounds like it means business."

"I don't wanna go. I didn't see all the falls yet," Josh whined.

"You'll get to do that another day," April assured him.

"What a baby!" Mandy muttered.

Another peal of thunder shook the ground, persuading even Josh it was time to leave.

They hurried toward the lodge to stabbing flashes of lightning and almost constant thunder.

Toni soon found she had turned her left ankle and fell behind. David dropped back and put his arm around her waist, enabling Toni to move somewhat faster.

A few hundred feet from their goal, a pelting rain sent the group sprinting for the safety of the verandah where they collapsed, gasping for breath. The children laughed, relishing the sport.

"I was afraid you might get caught in the rain," Evelyn said. After satisfying herself that the children were all right, she shook her head over Toni's disheveled state. Bits of pine straw and twigs clung to her dress and legs, and Toni felt a streak of mud on her forehead. "I suppose I shouldn't ask what happened to you," Evelyn said with a wry grin.

David's unexpected smile twisted Toni's heart. "Nothing," he said. "Miss Schmidt just won a race."

She began to shiver, and April took her arm. "Come on, let's find some paper towels and dry off."

"She looks drownded," Josh offered.

"There isn't any 'ded' in drowned," Mandy corrected.

❧

"Those are some kids David has," April said when she and Toni reached the privacy of the ladies' room. "They'll likely lead you a merry chase."

Toni glared at April. "Not me! They're not my responsibility."

"That's too bad. A little love would go a long way with those two."

April blotted rain from Toni's hair for a moment in silence. "David Trent seems to be a fine man. You should get to know him better and see where it leads."

"It wouldn't lead to the altar, if that's what you're thinking. You of all people should know how I feel about that."

"Yes, but I hoped by now you might realize how foolish the vow you made years ago really is," April said.

"It's not foolish to me."

"So you say. 'The lady doth protest too much, methinks.' "

Toni realized nothing she could say would change her friend's mind. "The lady hath a headache, and methinks she needs go home."

April smiled. "You whine almost as well as Josh. All right, brat—let's go."

Brat, indeed! Toni adopted an injured tone. "And you are supposed to be my friend."

"I am," April said sincerely. "And as your oldest and dearest friend, I hope you'll take my advice. Don't allow yourself to be afraid of David Trent."

"I'm not afraid of him." Toni's denial was quick, though not entirely accurate.

"Then prove it—let him into your life."

That night, reflecting on April's words, Toni thought it was just as well that the Winters were going back to Washington— and that Evelyn was leaving too.

With those matchmakers out of the way, dealing with David Trent would be a great deal easier.

twelve

In the last few days before leaving on her retirement cruise, Evelyn spent as much time as she could with David and the children, as well as making herself available for Toni. Although Evelyn had officially retired, she graciously made sure that Toni could handle everything that might come her way at the DHR.

The first few nights of that week, Toni came home to find David and the children there for supper. Along with food, Evelyn skillfully gave the children a few needed lessons in table manners—reminding Toni of her own similar experience as Evelyn's ward. Toni learned that Evelyn also took them to the offices of her medical doctor and dentist, introduced them to the staff, and picked up new patient forms for David to fill out. "It'll save time to complete these now," she advised David. On every form, Toni was listed as the backup person to be notified in an emergency, since Evelyn wouldn't always be in town.

On Wednesday, Evelyn went with David to register the children in their new schools. Josh seemed impressed when David mentioned they would be in the same schools he had attended as a child.

That night at supper, Mandy aired a major complaint. "They start school too soon here. We didn't go back until after Labor Day in Virginia. It's not fair."

"That means you'll get out earlier next summer," Toni pointed out.

"The schools are all air conditioned now, so going back in August doesn't make any difference. Now, when I was in school. . . ," Evelyn began.

"Spare us the ancient history," David teased.

The night before Evelyn was to leave, David invited them to

come to the condo for his "killer chili," apparently the only main dish he knew how to make. Toni had a good excuse not to go, since Thursday night was the time for Community Church's fellowship supper, prayer meeting, and choir practice.

"Can't you play hooky one time?" Evelyn asked.

"We're getting some new music, and I really should be there. Besides, it's the last time you'll be with David and the children for awhile, and that should be a family time."

"It would be with you there. You may not realize it, but you're are as much a part of the Trent family as if you'd been born into it."

Perhaps to you, Evelyn. I doubt the other Trents would agree.

❧

After extensive planning, which involved the aid of David and several travel agents, Evelyn was finally about to fulfill her dream to travel to faraway places and Toni would truly be on her own at work. On the third Friday in August, Toni joined Evelyn on her front porch swing—now surrounded by her new luggage—and waited for David to arrive to take her to the Chattanooga airport.

Toni looked at the itinerary Evelyn had organized with her usual efficiency. Today she would fly to Miami, the port where her Caribbean cruise would begin. After the cruise, Evelyn would travel cross-country by train to spend some time in California with her recently widowed college roommate. Both planned to fly to Hawaii for two weeks before touring New Zealand and Australia, finally returning to California six weeks later.

"From there I'll decide where to go next," Evelyn said.

"Surely you'll be ready to come home by then."

"That remains to be seen. I have a lot of years of staying home to make up for. I still want to see the Canadian Rockies and Yosemite and Yellowstone, for starters."

"I knew you planned to travel, but I wish you could have waited until I felt more secure in your job."

"It's your job now, and having me around would be a

crutch you don't need. For that reason, it's providential that the cruise leaves so soon."

"I'm sure David wishes you'd stay longer too. When you get tired of living out of suitcases, we'll be glad to have you back."

Evelyn smiled faintly. "That's at least one thing you'll be doing together." She glanced at her watch. "Speaking of David, he should be here by now."

As if on cue, David's silver truck pulled up to the curb. Three of its doors opened and the children jumped out onto the walkway. *Evelyn's brother is punctual, if nothing else.*

David took the porch steps in a couple of strides and picked up Evelyn's largest bag. "It looks like you might be aiming to go somewhere."

The children scrambled onto the porch. Josh struggled to pick up the second suitcase, which Mandy tried to wrest from him. "You're not big enough to carry that," she scolded.

Josh stubbornly held on to one of the bag's handles. "I am too!"

"I'll take it." Toni settled the argument by carrying the bag to the truck. Toni felt a pleasant tingle when David took it from her, and once more she wondered if he felt it too.

"Thanks." David looked as if he wanted to say more, but he turned away to receive Evelyn's carry-on bag.

"I hope you can handle all this luggage by yourself," he said.

"Oh, yes—I practiced to make sure. The big suitcase has wheels and a pullout handle the others ride on. Quite efficient."

David secured the luggage in the truck bed, herded the children into the backseat, and opened the passenger door for Evelyn.

Her voice held a note of wonder. "I can't believe I'm really leaving."

Toni smiled. "It certainly looks that way."

"You have the list of people to call if anything goes wrong with the house?"

"Yes, and I'll make sure to pay the bills on time."

"Drive the sedan at least once a week—I left the key on my dresser."

"Don't worry about a thing. The house and car and the DHR office and I will all get along just fine."

Evelyn smiled ruefully. "Thanks for the reminder I'm not indispensable. Good-bye, Toni."

"Have a good flight and a wonderful cruise—and a fantastic adventure. Drop us a postcard now and then, okay?"

In a rare display of affection, Evelyn hugged Toni and David in turn before he helped her into the truck and closed the door.

"I'm sorry you can't go with us," David told Toni.

I'm not. "The DHR calls," she said.

He glanced into the backseat. "All buckled up? Good. Let's hit the road."

Toni stepped back from the curb and waved. After David's truck rounded the corner and disappeared from sight, she went back inside.

Suddenly, the house seemed very empty. *Everything looks the same, yet so much has changed.* With Evelyn gone, Toni would have no one to turn to for help with the DHR office.

"You can handle it," Evelyn had assured Toni, and she wanted to believe it was so.

On the plus side, Evelyn won't be here to push David at me.

Toni wondered how much difference that would make. She hadn't forgotten Josh's question. Had David really promised they'd have another mother when they moved to Rockdale, or was it a case of a little boy's imagination?

Toni sighed. Josh and Mandy needed a mother, all right— but anyone who expected her to step into that role was sadly mistaken.

Toni picked up her briefcase and squared her shoulders. She faced a full day at the DHR office, and she didn't intend to start it by coming in late.

≈

Her generally warm reception in Rockdale had surprised and

heartened Toni, but she knew not everyone approved of her or would like her actions. Some thought she was too young for so much responsibility, while others would resent anyone who took Evelyn's place. That fact had become evident even before Evelyn left when Toni denied renewal of a day care center's license. The irate owner demanded that Evelyn Trent make the inspection herself, since her replacement obviously didn't know what she was doing.

Evelyn had set the woman straight in no uncertain terms; but now she was gone, leaving Toni to fight her own battles.

"You can't waver," Evelyn told Toni. "Stick to your guns and never allow anyone to intimidate you. I know you can do it."

Yes, but only with the help of the Lord, Toni realized, in this as in everything else. Otherwise, she would surely fail.

"Mrs. Norris wants you to call her," Anna said when Toni walked in the door.

"Did she say why?"

"She wants a reinspection—she says she's 'taken care of the so-called deficiencies' in your report."

"I have a custody meeting this morning and a foster home visit after lunch. Tell her I'll get there when I can."

Despite its occasional headaches, Toni liked her work and the sense of accomplishment that came with helping someone. Pleased that the day had gone well, she locked the office door shortly after five o'clock and started walking home. The nearer she got, the more her thoughts turned to Evelyn—and David.

No doubt David is back by now. I'm sure Evelyn made it to the airport on time. She'll call tonight, so there's no need for me to contact David.

As she reached the porch, Toni heard the telephone ringing. She dug out her door key and hurriedly unlocked the door, which David had repaired as promised. She was a bit breathless when she answered, and even more so when she heard David's voice.

"I thought I'd given you time to get home, but it sounds like you had to run to the phone."

"I just got here—it's been a busy day. Did Evelyn get away all right?"

"Yes, the plane left almost on time. We haven't been back long ourselves. Evelyn asked me to bring over a gift she got for you, then I thought we might grab some food."

Toni listened in silence, suspecting more of Evelyn's matchmaking behind the "gift" and supper invitation. "That's very kind, but you've already had a long day. You don't have to bring the gift over tonight." *And you most certainly don't have to feed me.*

"Oh, but I do," David insisted. "I promised Evelyn I'd deliver it right away. The kids like barbecue, so we can swing by your place on the way to Pitt's Place. You might as well go with us."

Evelyn no doubt told him how much I like that barbecue. "I haven't eaten at Pitt's Place in years," she admitted.

"Neither have I. I'll be there in fifteen minutes."

David hung up before Toni had a chance to reply. She started to call him back to tell him not to come, but that seemed rather foolish. Since David was determined to come by anyway, she would wait until he arrived to tell him she wasn't going with them.

Toni changed into chino slacks and a comfortable knit top. She ran a comb through her hair and went to the front porch to wait for the now familiar silver truck to pull up to the curb.

Minutes later, Josh scrambled out of the pickup and ran up onto the porch, holding out a clumsily wrapped package. "This is for you."

"We didn't get it wrapped very well," Mandy said as she and her father climbed the steps.

David handed her an envelope. "This goes with it."

Toni scanned Evelyn's brief note:

Toni—This is for your desk.

"Open it, Toni," urged Josh.

Toni removed the wrapping to reveal a polished mahogany

desk nameplate, with TONI SCHMIDT, DIRECTOR lettered in gold script.

"It's beautiful, but why didn't Evelyn give it to me before she left?"

"She ordered it from a store in Chattanooga a few weeks ago, and it just came in. We picked it up on the way home."

"I didn't expect anything like this," Toni said.

"I suppose Evelyn thought it might make you feel more in charge," David said. "Now that it's been delivered, we can go to Pitt's Place."

"I don't think I ever said I was going," Toni said.

David seemed surprised. "Of course you are. Put your gift away, and we'll be on our way."

Toni was aware that the children were watching as if waiting to see if she would give in. *David needs to know he can't just order me around. I should stay here and prove that point.*

But she had to eat sometime, anyway, and she sure liked Pitt's barbecue. After all, hadn't Jeremy Winter warned her not to cut off her nose to spite her face?

"I'll be back in a minute," she said.

thirteen

"Pitt's Place seems to be popular as ever," Toni commented when David pulled into the graveled parking lot. Many of the cars and pickups parked haphazardly around the ancient frame building bore license plates from nearby Alabama counties, with a smattering from nearby Tennessee and Georgia.

Mandy read the sign over the front entrance aloud. " 'The best ribs and pulled pork in the world.' Is it really that good?"

"You can judge that for yourself," David said.

"Wow, look at all these people!" exclaimed Josh.

"From the size of the crowd, we'll have a long wait to get a table," said Toni.

David eased the truck into a narrow space between a new luxury car and a battered pickup. "If you don't mind eating it at home, I can order at the takeout counter."

Toni was about to tell him they could wait for a table when she noticed several of the people standing near the entrance were drinking beer. When she was a teenager, Pitt's Place had not sold beer. From her own bitter experience, she knew that kind of atmosphere was not fit for children. "Yes, that would be better."

"I know what the kids want. What about you, Toni?"

"I always liked the pulled pork barbecue plate special with sides of beans and slaw—no fries."

"If they have it, you'll get it. Sit tight, kids. This could take awhile."

Josh called after his father. "Hurry up fast! I'm hungry."

"You're always hungry," Mandy said with disdain.

"Josh is a growing boy," Toni commented.

"I don't know where," Mandy said. "He eats and eats and

stays skinny. I'd be too fat to get in the door if I ate half of what he does."

Josh giggled. "Mandy, Mandy, two by four, can't get through the kitchen door," he singsonged.

His sister jabbed him in the ribs with her elbow. "That's not funny."

"Ow, that hurt!" Josh flailed at her with open hands, and Toni decided it was time to intervene.

"Stop that, you two!"

Both stopped hitting to stare at Toni in surprise, then Josh burst into tears.

"I wanna go hooooome," he howled.

So do I. I wonder what would happen if I howled too?

"We'll be going home in a few minutes," Toni said instead.

Josh quit sobbing and raised his head. "Not that home—I mean home to Virginia."

"I know you miss your friends, but you'll make new ones here."

Mandy sounded as if she might be on the verge of tears too. "Nana Alice and Larry aren't here."

She might not ask David anything personal, but she welcomed the opportunity to learn about their grandparents from the children. "How long did you live with them?"

"Forever and forever," Josh said dramatically.

Mandy spoke impatiently. "You don't know anything. We went to live with Nana Alice when Daddy had to go out of the country to someplace we couldn't go with him. I was halfway through the second grade then."

"Nana Alice needed a daddy, so she got Larry."

"Larry is her husband, Dum—" Mandy caught herself just in time.

Toni knew she shouldn't pump the children for information, but she wondered how much David really knew about their situation.

"Did you like Larry?"

"Larry marry, scary Larry," Josh sang.

"Larry isn't scary," Mandy corrected.

"Do you like him?"

The moment Toni spoke, she realized she had probed too much. The rays of the late summer afternoon streamed through the truck's open windows and highlighted the stubborn set of Mandy's chin. Her body language spoke her thoughts with silent clarity: *It's none of your business, Nosy Miss Toni.*

"Mommy didn't like Larry," Josh offered. "That's why she told Daddy—"

Mandy quickly covered her brother's mouth. "You know what Daddy says about talking ugly about people."

Josh slapped at Mandy's hand, and she took it away. "Ouch! That hurt! 'Sides, I wasn't talking ugly."

"No, but you were about to."

"Let's not start a fight," Toni said quickly.

"She hits me all the time," Josh complained.

"I do not! You're always hollering, then I get the blame."

They squabbled on for a few more minutes until Josh remembered that he was hungry and started whining again.

Mandy sighed. "Maybe you should go see what's taking Daddy so long," she suggested to Toni.

I wouldn't dare leave you and Josh alone—you might hurt each other, Toni imagined herself telling Mandy. *If they were my children—*

Toni stopped the thought in its tracks. *They are not mine, and they are not my responsibility.* However, she would still treat them with patience and respect. "You can see how crowded the place is. It takes the kitchen help awhile to get so many orders put together, but it shouldn't be much longer now."

Toni hoped she sounded confident, but she was hungry too. It had been hours since the scant lunch she'd eaten at her desk, and the tantalizing aroma of smoke rising from the open hickory wood pit made her stomach rumble.

"Maybe Daddy will let us eat in the truck," Josh said.

"Not hardly." Mandy looked at Toni almost defiantly. "The condo is a mess. I don't think you'd want to eat there."

"We can go to Toni's house," Josh said. "House, mouse!"

Toni smiled at the boy's mercurial mood change. "I don't have a mouse in my house," she said.

"Where Nana Alice lives, they say 'There's a moose in the hoose, get it oot,'" Mandy said.

"That sounds like the Tidewater regional accent. I've heard some Canadians talk that way too."

Mandy and Josh stared at Toni as if she were speaking Urdu. *There I go, saying stupid things again.* She was glad to see David striding across the parking lot with their food.

"Hey, crew, did you think I wasn't coming back?"

"I thought Toni should go inside and see what was happening," Mandy said.

David glanced at Toni, who quickly focused her attention on stowing the carryout sacks around her feet. "The food smells wonderful," she said.

"We're gonna go to Toni's house to eat," Josh announced when David started the truck's engine.

David cast a sidelong glance at Toni and smiled. "Thanks for the invitation—I'm afraid our place isn't fit for company just now."

I didn't invite you. Although it was the truth, Toni knew it would sound ungracious to say so. "No problem," she said.

"This reminds me of old times," David said a few minutes later when they entered Evelyn's kitchen. "I wish I had a dime for every meal I've eaten at this table."

After the children washed their hands, Toni asked them to set the table with the everyday stoneware, aware that flimsy paper plates would be no match for the ribs and barbecue. Their hunger made them finish the task quickly. David poured milk for the children and opened cans of soda for himself and Toni. When everyone was seated, Toni glanced at David questioningly.

He looked back and answered her unspoken question. "Our hostess will bless the food," he said.

Another presumption that bordered on a command. But this was one order Toni did not intend to dispute.

"All right. Let's pray." Mindful that the children watched her closely, Toni folded her hands and bowed her head. "Dear Lord, thank You for this day and all its blessings and for this food. May it strengthen our bodies and fit us to do Your service. In Jesus' name, amen."

"Now can we eat?" Josh asked plaintively.

Laughing, David put a slab of ribs on the boy's plate. "Have at it, little buddy."

Toni transferred Mandy's food to a plate and served herself last. The children were too busy eating to tease or fight with one another, and she and David savored their own food in quiet appreciation. As they ate, the thought occurred to Toni that anyone who didn't know better might think these four belonged together in this place.

We look like a family.

Almost as soon as Toni acknowledged that thought, she canceled it with another: *This is David Trent's family, not mine. I do not belong to him, and this is not our house.*

"What's for d'ert?" asked Josh, who had put away an amazing amount of ribs and fries but spurned the accompanying coleslaw.

"Dirt?" Toni repeated.

"He means 'dessert,'" Mandy supplied.

"I don't know where you'll put it, but I have store-bought cookies and chocolate ice cream. Will that do?"

David pretended surprise. "What, no homemade goodies?"

"Like we ever have any at our house," Mandy said.

The girl's tone was a bit too saucy to suit Toni, but since David said nothing, she would not make an issue of it herself. "Trust me, they're better than nothing, which is what you'd have if you waited for me to bake cookies in this hot weather."

"Help Toni clear the table first," David told the children. "What about the dishes?" he asked Toni.

"They go in the dishwasher—you don't have to rinse them first. I'll get the ice cream while you're doing that."

"We didn't have a dishwasher when I was growing up,"

David said. "That was the first thing Evelyn added when she remodeled the kitchen."

"You mean you had to wash dishes by hand?" Mandy asked in mock horror.

"Yes. And even worse, when I was your age we didn't have a color television set."

Toni entered into the spirit of his banter. "I'm sure your father also walked five miles to school each way through snowdrifts tall as this roof."

Josh's eyes grew round. "I don't wanna walk to school. I don't wanna go to school. I wanna go back hoome."

Mandy regarded her brother with disgust. "Toni was just teasing. You never really had to do anything like that in Alabama, did you, Daddy?"

David shook his head. "No, and neither will you, Josh. Remember that walk we took to your school the other day? It's five minutes away, not five miles."

"Ugh. Don't talk about school," said Mandy.

Toni handed each of the children a bowl of ice cream, wishing she'd thought through her comment before opening her mouth. "Here's your d'ert," she told Josh. "When you finish it, I have something to show you."

David looked interested. "What is it?"

"You'll see," Toni said. "Anybody want a cookie?"

"I'll take two, store-bought or not," David said.

When they finished eating, Toni invited David to sit on the living room couch between Josh and Mandy.

"What happens next?" he asked.

Toni took Evelyn's photograph album from the shelf and handed it to David. "I thought the children might like to see the pictures Evelyn has of some of their relatives," she said.

David opened the album to the first page. "I haven't seen these pictures in years. That one's of Grandpa and Grandma Trent on their golden wedding anniversary—you're named for him, Josh. Those are my parents—your grandparents, kids—when they got married."

"Their clothes look funny," Mandy remarked.

"Yours will look peculiar to your grandchildren one of these days too," David said.

Mandy wrinkled her nose. "I won't ever be that old," she said.

"That's me!" Josh exclaimed when David turned the page.

Without comment, Mandy looked at the picture of their mother holding Josh.

"Remember why you aren't smiling in this one?" David asked.

"I guess I didn't want to be a big sister."

"I heard you'd just lost your front teeth," Toni said.

"Or your last friend," David said. He turned the page. "You look a lot happier in these."

"Is that Mommy? She looks sad," Josh said.

"You were too little to notice, but she was already sick then," Mandy said matter-of-factly.

"I miss Mommy," Josh said. Tears came into his eyes, and Toni felt her heart constrict when David hugged his son close, then put his other arm around Mandy.

They all need the Comforter. If only David understood how to fill the void in their lives—

David closed the photo album and stood. "We'd better be getting home. Thanks for the use of your kitchen." David's countenance suggested he could have done without that walk down memory lane.

"And thanks to you for furnishing the food." *I didn't intend to make you feel sad,* she hoped her expression conveyed.

Toni followed them out onto the front porch. In the deep summer twilight, Venus hung on the horizon, surrounded by a few bright stars. "God has given us another beautiful night," she said.

Josh looked puzzled. "I thought the weatherman did that."

David seemed to suppress a smile. "The men you see on television report what their charts show. They don't make the weather."

"Nobody does that," Mandy said. "Weather just happens."

"Get in the truck, kids," David ordered, and each tried to be the first.

"Your children have some interesting notions," Toni said. "I agree with Evelyn—it's time you started taking them to Sunday school."

David regarded her levelly. "And I think you're beginning to sound like my sister." He started toward the truck, then turned back briefly. "Good night, Toni—I'll call tomorrow."

fourteen

Toni arose early Saturday and went to the sunroom for her daily quiet time. The morning was still cool, and she raised the windows to get a better look at the birds congregating around the backyard feeder. A pair of robins splashed in the ancient stone birdbath until a scolding blue jay swooped down, temporarily scattering them and causing several finches to rise in unison from their perches on the feeder. At the tip of the tallest pine tree in the yard, a mockingbird burst into song.

At times such as this, Toni wondered how anyone could view these marvels of God's creation and still deny His existence. It never ceased to amaze her that God had always loved her, even when she scarcely knew He existed. She recalled the words she had sung so recently: *His eye is on the sparrow, and I know He watches me. . .*

Toni opened her prayer journal to a blank page. She usually listed her concerns rather quickly. This morning, however, she sat still for a long time before she began to write.

David's children need spiritual help, and I can't turn my back on them. I suspect their father does too, but I don't want him to misunderstand how I feel about him.

Toni put down her pen and gazed into the distance without really seeing anything. If she had to characterize the way she felt about David Trent, it might be summed up in a single word: confused.

Toni sighed. Through the years, she had gone out with a number of men on casual dates that never developed into anything more. She had worked with still others she considered her friends. Yet, no man had ever so instantly appealed to her or had been more difficult to ignore than David Trent. Toni had resolved to shut him out of her life completely—

until she saw him again and met his children.

This isn't getting me anywhere. She put the prayer journal aside and opened her daily devotional guide. The day's Scripture—Proverbs 3:5—all but leaped at her from the page: "Trust in the Lord with all thine heart; and lean not unto thine own understanding."

Maybe that's what I've been doing—depending on my own weak understanding.

Toni bowed her head in earnest prayer. *I don't understand what I should do, and I know I can't handle this alone. Give me Your understanding, Lord, so I can help David's children.*

❧

The telephone remained silent throughout Saturday morning as Toni went about her usual chores. David had said he would call, but when he had not done so by one o'clock, Toni decided her comment about taking the children to church had probably made him shy away.

In any case, Toni was not sorry she'd said it. Evelyn wasn't there to set her brother straight, and somebody needed to do it. On that point, at least, she felt no confusion. She was debating whether to call and tell him so when the phone finally rang.

David spoke without preamble. "Hi, Toni. Ready to go for a bike ride?"

He sounded friendly, and Toni decided that if he harbored any ill feelings, he certainly hid them well.

"I've been working at home all morning, and I still have to buy groceries," she said.

"You can do that later. This is the last weekend before school starts, and the kids haven't had a chance to ride their bikes any distance at all since we got here. We hope you'll join us and show us an easy ride."

Toni hesitated briefly. "I'll make a deal with you. I'll ride with you and the children today if you'll promise to take them to church tomorrow."

David sounded amused. "You drive a hard bargain."

"Take it or leave it."

"I suspect my sister's hand in this, but I agree to your terms. Can you be ready in half an hour?"

"Yes—and thanks for asking."

This time Toni hung up first, savoring her small victory. Instead of telling her when he would be there, David had given Toni some say in the arrangements.

David Trent is learning—even if I don't want to be his teacher.

❧

"Where to?" David asked when he had added Toni's bike to the other three in the truck bed.

"Josh and I should start with an easy trail. How about the top of Warren Mountain?"

"I hiked around it some as a kid, but I never took my bike there," David said.

"April and I often rode all the way to the top. It was one of our favorite places."

"Isn't Warren Road where she and the congressman live when they're in town?"

"Yes. Their house is about a quarter of the way up the hill, before the road gets so steep. The top of the mountain is almost flat."

"All right—next stop, Warren Mountain."

David turned onto Warren Road and passed Ted and Janet Brown's apartment complex, then the entrance to an expensive, gated subdivision. "I can't believe all this new development," David said.

"The area has changed a lot, but I hope Warren Mountain itself will stay undeveloped." She pointed out the ridge ahead. "That's where we're going," she told the children.

On the other side of the Winters' house, the road steepened and began to twist and turn on its way to the summit.

"I wouldn't want to ride my bike up here," Mandy said.

"I would," said Josh.

Mandy spoke with scorn. "You have trouble pedaling five feet on the sidewalk. You can't climb a hill."

"Yes, I can!"

"Can't!"

David turned and gave both children a warning glance, then he spoke to Josh. "It's not entirely a matter of strength. Your bike doesn't have gears, and it would be hard for anyone to ride uphill without them."

The boy still looked downcast, and Toni tried to reassure him. "Don't worry, Josh—you can ride your bike just fine where we're going."

"I'd forgotten how great the view is from up here," David said when the road leveled out. From the western summit of Warren Mountain, Rockdale looked like a miniature village nestled against the larger backdrop of Lookout Mountain.

"Turn at the amphitheater sign. You can leave the truck in the parking lot," Toni said.

Moments later, the children raced to the edge of the shallow amphitheater and peered down at the rows of seats that had been cut from the rock of the largely undeveloped eastern side of Warren Mountain.

"This place wasn't here when I was growing up. What's it used for?" asked David.

"Mostly bluegrass concerts and fiddling contests in the fall and spring. Community Church holds a sunrise service here every Easter. Seeing the Resurrection story unfold just as the sun comes up over that bluff is breathtaking. The children should see it next Easter."

Toni took David's nod to mean that he would at least consider it. "Come on, kids. Put on your helmets. We're about to do some serious bike riding."

The logging road Toni remembered bicycling on with April more than a decade ago was now so overgrown they were forced to ride single file. Toni led the way, followed by Mandy then Josh, with David bringing up the rear. With every turn of the wheels, Toni remembered why she enjoyed riding so much, and even Josh, although his steering was a bit erratic, kept up and rode well.

Toni tried to lead them around the roughest areas, but the

going was far from smooth.

"I take it loggers don't use this road anymore," David said.

"No one does. The original timber stands were exhausted years ago. The Warrens replanted the slopes, and if Jeremy Winter has anything to say about it, they'll never be clear-cut."

It was cool at the top of the mountain, especially in the places where trees on either side of the trail met to form a shadowy canopy. The riders dodged an occasional fallen limb, as well as thorns from the blackberry and winterberry bushes that grew at the road's edge.

At one point they encountered a swarm of persistent gnats. "It's a good thing we put the bug stuff on before we started out," David said.

Josh made a face. "Bugs taste yucky."

"You're not supposed to eat them," Mandy said with disdain. "Anyway, they can't get in if you keep your mouth closed for a change."

"Then close yours," Josh said.

Although Toni expected David to reprove the children, he remained silent, and she decided he must have chosen to ignore all but their worst arguments.

A bit farther on, they encountered a stretch so wet they had to walk their bikes around several mud puddles.

"I'm tired," Josh whined after a few steps.

I wondered how long it would take him to start that. Aloud, Toni assured him a beautiful clearing lay ahead. "It's on the right, not very far away. We'll stop there for a break."

"I don't see anyplace like that," Mandy said after awhile.

They had reached a dry stretch of the logging track, and Toni got back on her bicycle. "Let's ride on a little farther. I'm sure we're almost there."

"I'm tired," Josh whined.

Mandy didn't sound much better. "Look how these briars are scratching my legs."

David looked at Toni. *You obviously don't know where you're going,* she read in his expression. "Maybe I should mount a scouting patrol," he said.

Why did I ever agree to do this? Toni wondered.

Josh shrieked as if he'd already been abandoned. "Don't go, Daddy! Don't leave!"

Something rustled in the underbrush and Mandy screamed. "Is that a rattlesnake? I don't like snakes."

A lone chipmunk scampered across the path, and David laughed. "There's your snake, Mandy."

While looking to see where the chipmunk went, Toni caught a glimpse of green and walked her bike toward it. "There's the clearing—it was just a little farther than I remembered."

They entered the small, grassy meadow—now bright with purple asters and yellow black-eyed Susans—where Toni and April had often rested when they rode up Warren Mountain.

Mandy leaned her bike against an oak tree and stood still, listening. "I hear something."

"So do I," said Josh.

"Sounds like water." David glanced at Toni. "It's the Warren spring, isn't it?"

Toni nodded. "Let's go see it."

On the other side of a gap in the trees, water fell a few feet from a cleft in a small ridge and splashed into a rock-lined pool before joining a narrow stream.

Josh clapped his hands in delight. "It's a little waterfall!"

"Where does the water come from?" Mandy asked.

"There's an everlasting spring just behind those rocks," Toni said. "You remember meeting Kincaid and Warren Winter. A long time ago, their ancestors got all their water here."

David put his hand into the flowing stream issuing from the rock. "It's ice cold."

"I'm thirsty. I want a drink," Josh whined.

"The spring water is probably safe to drink, but I think we should use the bottles we brought with us," Toni said.

"I'm hot," Mandy complained.

"April and I used to take off our shoes and put our feet in the pool to cool off," Toni said.

Josh jumped up and down, his fatigue temporarily forgotten. "I wanna do that. Can I, Daddy?"

"I suppose so." David looked at Toni, his expression clear: *This is your idea, so you can carry it out.*

"Sit down and I'll help you take off your shoes and socks," Toni directed.

Josh tugged vainly at one of his sneakers. "I can do it by myself!"

"Not likely," said Mandy. "I made sure to tie the strings tight, then I double knotted them."

David knelt in front of his son. "Here, Buddy, I'll help you."

When Josh allowed him to do so without protest, Toni detected a gleam of victory in Mandy's eyes. *I won,* her look seemed to say. *You're not the boss of us.*

"How about you?" David asked Toni. "Want to take off your shoes and join the kids?"

Toni shook her head. "No, thanks. I'll get the water bottles."

"I'll help you carry them." David gave the children a stern look. "Don't budge an inch. I'll be right back."

"Hurry up! I'm thirsty!" Josh called after them.

"I don't suppose they'll drown while we're gone," David said.

"I'm afraid not."

David looked at Toni and spoke with the same ironic tone. "So the truth comes out. You really don't like kids, after all."

Embarrassed, Toni busied herself with retrieving Mandy's water bottle. "You know that's not true."

"I'd like to think so." David put his hand, still cold from the spring water, on hers. Toni shivered at his touch, not wholly from the cold. Once more, he regarded her with the intent, yet guarded, expression she did not understand.

"I care enough to want them to be in church tomorrow."

David removed his hand and stepped back. "That again," he said flatly.

Toni lifted her chin. "Yes. I know you went to First Church when you were growing up. Your children deserve the same foundation."

"I know who told you that, but the truth is I haven't set foot inside First in years."

"That doesn't matter. My friend Mary Oliver teaches Sunday school. She'll be glad to see that Josh and Mandy get put into the proper groups."

"I don't know," David said. "The children aren't used to going to Sunday school."

"All the more reason to take them."

"That's what Evelyn said."

"You promised," Toni reminded him.

"I agreed to take them to church. I didn't say where. I suppose Community has Sunday school classes too?"

Toni felt mixed emotions. Getting Josh and Mandy into Bible study was a step in the right direction, but she had expected they would go to First. The prospect of seeing them at her church every Sunday was a bit daunting. "Yes, the church has a full program for all age groups."

David gave her a peculiar look. "You won't mind having them there?"

"Of course not. I just wish—"

Josh's plaintive cry interrupted Toni. "I'm still thirrrsty!"

"Water's on the way," David called back.

Mandy regarded them suspiciously when they returned. "What took you so long?"

David handed the children their water bottles. "We were making plans for tomorrow."

Josh groaned. "I don't wanna ride bikes again!"

"Me, neither," said Mandy.

"We won't. You're going to Toni's church for Sunday school tomorrow."

Mandy rolled her eyes but said nothing.

"Are you gonna be there?" Josh asked Toni.

Mandy muttered something under her breath that Toni thought sounded like "I hope not," which David apparently did not hear.

"My feet are cold," Josh said.

"Mine too," added Mandy.

"I'll get something to dry them with," David said.

Toni was surprised. "You brought a towel?"

"Sure. I also have a first aid kit in my bike saddlebag. I told you I was a Boy Scout."

❧

While the children were putting on their shoes, Toni glanced at her watch. "If everyone's had enough riding, I need to get back to town and do some shopping."

"I think we're all ready to leave," David said, tucking the damp hand towel into his saddlebag.

"If you go on a few hundred yards west, you'll see the main road," Toni told David. "It's—"

"I know where we are now," he interrupted. "The road's steep, but quicker than going back the way we came. I'll get the truck and meet you at the road."

"Hurry up, Daddy," Josh said. "I'm hungry."

"You're impossible," Mandy said.

And so are you, Toni might have added.

Yet, in spite of it all, Toni admitted she really cared about David's children.

It must be because I see myself as a child in them, Toni told herself. *David Trent certainly has nothing to do with it.*

fifteen

After Toni finished her shopping and had a late supper, she got a telephone call from Mary Oliver. They chatted for awhile, then Mary asked Toni to come to lunch after church on Sunday.

"Once school starts, there's no telling when we can get together again."

Toni thought of previous Sundays she and David had shared. He had not asked her to go anywhere after church with him this Sunday, but if he should, she now had a good excuse to refuse. It wouldn't hurt David Trent to understand she had a life of her own. "All right—I'll be there around twelve-thirty."

❧

Although Toni feared he might change his mind, David brought the children to Community Church for Bible study on Sunday. Toni met David outside the welcome center, where he turned the children over to Mark Elliott, Community Church's educational director.

"What now?" David asked.

"You can go with me to the Seekers class."

"If there's an entrance exam, I'm sunk. I haven't been in Sunday school for more than twenty years."

"This isn't an old-fashioned Sunday school—it's a very informal Bible study, and no one will hassle you. I've been only a few times myself, but everyone has made me feel welcome."

The Seekers met in a part of the fellowship hall close to the kitchen, where coffee, juice, and pastries were readily available. A dozen men and women were already there when Toni and David arrived. When Toni introduced David, she found he already knew several of them, including the group's leader, Greg Harmon, one of David's childhood friends.

Toni soon realized that God was answering her prayers for

114

David in ways she never imagined, from the fact that he knew the leader to the current Bible study topic. Toni noticed that David seemed intensely interested in Greg Harmon's opening words.

"The world is so full of suffering and grief that even Christians sometimes feel overwhelmed and discouraged and don't know where to turn. In the next few weeks, we're going to look at what the Bible says about why God allows suffering. We'll talk about handling grief brought on when we see others suffer, as well as from our own losses. Let's ask God to be with us now as we seek His answers."

Toni bowed her head and added her own prayer. *Lord, I thank You that David brought his children today. Help him take what he needs from this study.*

She did not pray for herself or her needs; at the moment, she wanted nothing more than God's peace for David and his children.

⁂

Toni had to leave for the choir room before the children got out of Bible study, but when the choir came in, she saw them sitting where David and Evelyn had been the month before. David sat between the children and nodded almost imperceptibly when he saw Toni watching them. She translated his expression as "We're here, as promised" and smiled in reply.

Mandy sat with her arms folded in an attitude of bored resignation, while Josh seemed to be interested in everything around him. He swiveled in his seat and craned his neck.

As the service continued, Toni found it difficult not to keep looking at them. Her gaze seemed attracted to David Trent like steel filings to a magnet, and nearly every time she stole a glance at him, Toni found him looking at her.

After the service, David and the children were waiting to one side when Toni reached the vestibule.

"You didn't sing," Mandy said almost accusingly.

"Daddy said you would sing," Josh added.

Toni looked at David, who shrugged an apology.

"I did sing—in the choir. I don't sing all by myself very many Sundays."

"That's too bad," said David.

Toni ignored David's compliment and turned to the children. "What about you? Who wants to tell me what you did in Bible study?"

"I do!" Josh exclaimed. "We had cookies and punch and learned a song about a little man named Zeekus and I drawed his picture." He held up a messy finger painting of a stick figure in a skeletal tree, which Toni took to represent his idea of Zacchaeus.

"You drew his picture," Mandy corrected.

Josh sighed, clearly exasperated. "That's what I just said."

"If you don't want people to think you're dumb, you have to learn to talk right," Mandy said. "It's drew, not drawed."

Toni suppressed a smile. *Mandy sounded just like me there for a second.*

"What about your class?" she asked Mandy.

"It was all right, I guess."

David and Toni exchanged a glance, confirming the obvious: for Mandy, that was high praise.

"Can we come back next week, Daddy?" asked Josh.

"Do you want to?"

Josh hopped up and down on first one foot, then the other. "Yes. I had fun."

Toni smiled. "I wish I had time to hear more about what you did, but I have to go now."

"Why?" asked Mandy.

"I'm having lunch with a friend."

David looked surprised and disappointed in turn. "I suppose we'll have to ask you sooner next time."

Next time, maybe you won't take me for granted.

Josh tugged at David's hand. "I'm hungry." His pitiful tone suggested he had not eaten in days.

Toni glanced at her watch, then at David. "I must be going. I'm really glad you all came today. I'll see you later."

She hurried to her SUV and inserted the key into the ignition, then her hand suddenly began to tremble.

David and the children had participated in Bible study and worship, which was what she had wanted for them.

Toni wasn't automatically having lunch with them, which was what she had wanted for herself. Both could be considered victories.

Why, then, did she feel so miserable?

≈

The first time Toni saw Mary Oliver's house, it seemed like a palace. She was sixteen then and still afraid of Mary's father. As the man who had allowed Evelyn Trent to become her guardian, Judge Oliver could have, with the stroke of a pen, sent Toni to reform school. Despite her past, he had allowed his daughter to befriend Toni and invite her to their home.

The Olivers' hundred-year-old white frame house contained eleven spacious, high-ceilinged rooms, including a separate servant's quarters. In Toni's teenaged eyes, the house was so elegant she could not imagine an ordinary mortal like herself living there.

Mary had soon set Toni straight about that. "This place is cold in the winter and hot in the summer, there isn't much closet space, and something's always falling apart or breaking down."

Even after Toni realized Evelyn Trent's cottage was much more comfortable, the Oliver house continued to represent both a luxury and a family tradition she could never claim for herself.

Now, years later, the house and its grounds seemed far smaller than Toni remembered them. She still admired the home's stately Victorian architecture and carefully tended landscaping, but Toni no longer envied Mary for living in it.

Toni had just parked her SUV when she heard a distant rumble of thunder and looked up to see a lone thunderhead building in the summer sky. Toni wondered where David might be taking the children to eat. Statum's, his favorite restaurant, did not open on Sunday. The country club served brunch, but David was not yet a member. She thought it unlikely he would return to DeSoto so soon—especially without her. *I should have told him about the buffet at—*

That thought was immediately replaced by another: *I am not responsible for where David Trent eats. He can certainly make his own dining decisions.*

Toni hurried down the brick walkway flanked by giant boxwoods. She breathed in their fragrance and resolved to have shrubs like that of her own someday.

Mary waited at the door. "Sounds like a storm's brewing—I'm glad you made it here before the rain."

"It's probably only a passing shower. Where's the judge?" Toni added, seeing only two places set at the dining room table.

"He and the Harrisons went to brunch at the country club, so we have the house to ourselves."

"I hope you didn't go to a lot of trouble on my account," Toni said.

"Not at all. I made chicken salad yesterday, and we're having it on a croissant with fresh fruit on the side."

"With your special iced tea." Toni pointed to the frosty pitcher on the sideboard. "I remember how much I liked it."

"It's brewed tea, mixed with sugar and orange juice and crushed mint. The mint gives it that special taste."

Mary brought out their plates, filled their glasses, offered a brief grace, and turned to Toni. "I'm surprised you've haven't already told me about David Trent."

Toni took a sip of her iced tea before replying. "There's nothing to tell."

"I hear that he's quite handsome."

"Who told you that?"

"Several people. You know how it is—any unattached man sends all the matchmakers into a tizzy. Rockdale doesn't have many widowers."

Toni laughed. "I know. Evelyn has her own opinion of women who bombard widowers with so many cakes and casseroles they have to marry again in self-defense."

"Have you been making cakes and casseroles for David Trent?"

"Of course not. Evelyn asked me to help him with the children, and that's it."

"According to Jenny Suiter, it's all over town that Evelyn Trent's brother is spending a lot of time with her former ward."

"She probably started that story in the first place. Gossips like to make much ado about nothing."

Mary did not sound convinced. "Yes, but where there's smoke there might be fire, right?"

"Wrong—especially when there isn't even any smoke."

Mary was still skeptical. "Time will tell about that."

Toni seized the opportunity to change the subject. "Speaking of time, you don't have much free time left before you go back to work, do you?"

"None, actually. I've spent the last few days getting my classroom ready, and tomorrow all the Rockdale teachers gather for a joint meeting. We'll work in our schools on Tuesday, then our little darlings arrive on Wednesday."

The thought of teaching a roomful of Joshes made Toni shake her head. "I don't see how you do it."

"Sometimes, neither do I. Teaching is my calling, but that doesn't mean it's always easy."

"Josh Trent will be starting the first grade," Toni said. "I hope his teacher will be patient with him."

"So do I." Mary paused, then smiled. "I saw the class lists Friday. Josh Trent is in my room."

Toni smiled and clasped her hands together. "That's an answer to prayer! His father will be happy to know that Josh will be in such good hands."

Mary's tone was faintly sarcastic. "I'm sure you can't wait to share the good news with him."

"No. He'll find it out for himself. Now, not to change the subject, but I'd like to have the recipe for this excellent chicken salad."

"The way to a man's heart—"

"I told you I'm not interested in going there," Toni insisted.

She had no sooner spoken than a bright flash of light illuminated the sky, followed by thunder that rattled the house.

Both women jumped, and Mary laughed, "Somebody must think you're not telling the truth."

"You of all people should know I'm not interested in getting a man," Toni said.

Mary nodded. "I know what your mouth says, but I'm not sure your heart still believes it. You can fool other people, Toni, but don't try to fool yourself."

"I'm not."

Or are you? a nagging inner voice asked Toni.

sixteen

For the next few days, her work at the DHR office kept Toni too busy to think about much else. However, throughout the day on Wednesday, she wondered how the children were getting along on their first day in their Rockdale schools. She was reluctant to call David, but she reasoned it would be all right if she asked to speak to the children.

Soon after she came in from work, Toni had her hand on the telephone to call them when it rang. She let it ring twice again before she picked up the receiver.

David spoke with his usual directness. "Ready for a school report?"

"Is it a good one?"

"Let's say the reviews are mixed. I promised the kids takeout pizza tonight in honor of the occasion. If you like, I'll come by for you after I pick it up."

Toni hesitated. As much as she would like to talk to the children, she did not want to appear to assume the status of a member of the family. "Thanks for the invitation, but perhaps that's something you and the children should share."

"We will, but having a friend there will make it even better."

A friend? *David must not have seen the way Mandy looks at me—and Josh is usually too busy whining and hanging on to his father to pay much attention to anyone else.* Toni suppressed an ironical laugh.

"I didn't know the children thought of me as their friend."

"If they don't they should—anyway, please say you'll join us."

"All right, but you don't have to come by for me."

"It's not out of the way—I can be at your place around six o'clock."

Toni felt an edge of irritation. *There David goes again,*

telling me what he's going to do, rather than listening to me.

Toni's tone made her meaning clear. "If I come at all, I will drive myself." *Take it or leave it.*

David sounded genuinely puzzled. "Hey, if that's what you want, I don't have a problem with it. I was just trying to make it easier for you to say yes."

"I appreciate your concern, but your condo isn't exactly at the ends of the known earth, and I know how to get there. What time should I arrive?"

David was silent for a moment. "If you won't let me pick you up, come about a quarter of six. You can visit with the kids while I go for the pizza."

Considering the way they had behaved in the pizza restaurant, Toni would not be surprised if David did not want them anywhere near it again, especially when she was available to baby-sit.

"I'll do my best to keep them from hurting each other," Toni promised.

She sensed David's smile. "I hope that won't be necessary. You may be surprised how this day at school has affected them."

Pleasantly surprised, Toni hoped.

 za

With punctuality that matched David's, Toni reached David's condo a few minutes early. He came to the door with his truck keys in hand and seemed genuinely happy to see her.

"I asked the kids to set the table while I'm gone, so we can get right down to eating when I get back."

"Honk your horn when you get here, and we'll open the door for you," Toni said.

"That's my job!" said Josh.

"Sounds like you've had takeout pizza before."

"Among other stuff," Mandy said, with the tone of one growing weary of fast food.

At the door, David paused. "Thanks for coming tonight," he said privately to Toni. "Behave yourselves," he called to the children.

Toni closed the door behind David and turned to survey the condo's interior. "The last time I was here, boxes were stacked everywhere. I'm sure it took a lot of hard work to get it all unpacked and put away. It looks as if you've always lived here."

"It doesn't feel that way," Mandy said.

"I know," Toni said. "It always takes awhile to get used to a new place."

Mandy regarded her with curiosity. "Daddy said you used to live in Atlanta. Rockdale must seem like a hick town compared to it."

Toni smiled. "If I had grown up in a big city I might feel that way, but I like a smaller town."

"My new teacher said she went to school with you," Josh said, his tone suggesting doubt.

"Yes, Mary Oliver and I graduated from Rockdale High School the same year." Toni decided not to add that his teacher was her good friend.

"Miss Mary's a lot bigger 'n you," Josh said.

"People come in all sizes. What they look like on the out-side has nothing to do with who they really are inside."

You're preaching again, Mandy's pained expression told Toni, and she realized Mandy had a point.

"We'd better get started on the table," Toni said. "Who wants to get out the plates?"

Mandy's tone questioned Toni's intelligence. "I do, of course, since I'm taller. Josh puts out the little stuff."

"It's good you're learning to help out." Toni had meant to pay the children a compliment, but the moment she spoke, she realized she merely sounded patronizing.

If I'm all they have as a friend, these two would probably say they don't need any enemies.

The table eventually got set, and Toni was pouring milk into their glasses when they heard a horn blast.

"There's Daddy!" Josh exclaimed.

"Open the door," Toni said, but Josh had done so almost

before she could finish speaking.

David entered carrying two boxes, quickly filling the room with the unmistakable aroma of freshly baked pizza. "Looks like everything's ready. Good job, gang."

"Wash your hands, Daddy," Josh said when David had set the boxes on the counter.

David noticed Toni's amusement. "We help remind each other of these important things."

A few minutes later when they were seated around the table, Toni was heartened to see the children apparently waiting for grace to be said without being told.

David pointed to Josh. "It's your turn tonight, big boy."

Josh looked from him to Toni and back again. "Do I have to?"

"It's your turn," David repeated.

Josh sighed and put his hands together. "All right, but everybody has to close their eyes. No peeking."

"We're not playing hide-and-seek," Mandy murmured.

When Josh was satisfied with their attention, he prayed. "God is great. God is good. Let us thank-Him-for-our-food-amen." After speeding through the last portion, he glanced at Toni as if seeking her approval.

"Very good," she said.

"You might make a good auctioneer one of these days," David told Josh.

"What's a actioneer?" he asked.

David's mouth was full, so Mandy answered for him. "Auctioneer. That's a man who talks real fast when he sells things."

"Close enough," said David.

"Not all fast-talking salesmen are auctioneers, and some auctioneers are women," Toni observed.

Mandy rolled her eyes, obviously finding the conversation too boring for words.

"Have you told Toni about school yet?" David asked Mandy.

"There's nothing to tell," said Mandy. "Rockdale Middle School is just one big zero."

"Zero means nothing," Josh put in. "I learned that in kiddygardent."

"Kindergarten," David corrected automatically. He looked at Mandy. "Show Toni your class schedule. It doesn't look like a zero to me."

Mandy sighed in martyred resignation and pulled a wrinkled computer printout from her jeans pocket. Toni read aloud: "Amanda Jean Trent has home room with Mr. Bates; first hour, English with Mrs. Marshall; second hour, math with Mr. Barnes; third hour, physical education with Staff; fourth hour, lunch and social studies with Mrs. Franklin; fifth hour, study hall with Staff and sixth hour, activity period with Staff."

"That Staff must be one busy teacher," said David, but his attempt at humor failed to amuse his daughter.

" 'Staff' means I'll have a lot of substitutes until they hire more teachers."

"What about your other teachers?" asked Toni.

"They all look mean."

"Good," said David. "Mean teachers keep order, and you can't learn without an orderly classroom."

"How about the other students? Did you meet any potential friends?" Toni asked.

Mandy shook her head. "I'm the only new one in my home room, and probably in the whole school. Everybody else has known each other forever. One of the girls from the Bible study spoke to me in the hall, but we don't have any classes together."

"Give it a few days, and I'm sure you'll begin to make some friends."

Josh had been waiting impatiently for an opening in the conversation and now spoke. "I saw a new friend today."

"Who's that?" Toni asked.

"His name is Jeff. He was in my class at church."

"That must be Jeff Elliott," Toni said. "Tell me about your teacher."

"She said we could call her Miss Mary. She asked if we could tie our shoelaces. I told her I already know how to read, but she said she'd rather hear if we could tie our own shoes."

Mandy laughed. "Wow, are you going to be in trouble!"

"His sister has always tied Josh's shoes," David explained. "It didn't occur to me that it might not be best for him."

He spoke seriously, and Toni tried to hide her dismay. *Oh, David—how can a man so smart in so many ways be so clueless?*

Toni pulled a guess from thin air. "By this time next week, I predict you'll be tying your own shoes."

Josh looked hopeful. "Really?"

"Yes, but you'll have to practice a lot. Your sister will show you how, won't you, Mandy?"

"I've tried to, but little baby brother here always whined so much it was easier to do it for him."

"I don't whine," Josh whined, then looked surprised when everyone laughed.

"When you make a sound like that, you're whining," Toni said. "Now that you're a big first-grader, you can learn not to do it."

"Who's gonna teach me?"

"Nobody. You can do it for yourself."

"I'm too little," Josh wailed.

"You are not!" Mandy retorted. "You act like a baby just to get attention."

"I know you can quit whining if you want to." Toni caught David's eye. *Be patient with him, and he'll come around.*

David's expression reminded Toni of his son's plea: *I can't do this by myself. Help me, Toni.*

Toni returned her attention to Josh. "Tell me something else about your day," she invited.

Josh looked sad. "Everybody else's mommy brought them to school."

Toni's heart constricted. *I know how you must have felt, Josh. I wish you could have been spared that pain.*

"You know, it's very special to be the only one who had a daddy there," Toni told him.

Josh regarded her solemnly. "That's what Miss Mary said."

"I think Josh is fortunate to have such a wise teacher," David said.

Josh nodded and stretched out his arms. "Yeah, she's this wide."

"Daddy said wise, not wide!" Mandy corrected, and David and Toni fought to keep straight faces.

"She has a lot of rules too," Josh said.

"That's the way school is, Josh. Get over it," Mandy said.

Is there anything you like, Miss Negative? "Look for the good things—they're there," Toni said, but she doubted either child understood.

David stood and began collecting their plates, empty except for a few pieces of crust. "It's time to police the kitchen."

Mandy put the pizza boxes in the trash, and Josh collected the napkins while David loaded the dishwasher. When Toni started wiping the table and counters, she noticed David watching her with that strange expression she had never quite understood.

If David is thinking of me as a permanent part of his life because I can put up with his children and know my way around a kitchen, he's seriously mistaken. But how could she make him understand that without sounding presumptuous?

"Can I go to my room now?" Mandy asked when the kitchen was clean. "I want to write to Nana Alice."

"Yes, that would be a good thing for you to do. Tell her I said hello."

"You said I could watch my new tape," said Josh, not quite whining.

"And so you can. I'll set it up for you," David said.

"I can do it myself," Josh insisted.

"I'm sure you can, but I'll have to find it first." He turned to Toni. "Make yourself comfortable—I'll be right back."

Toni glanced at her watch. She had done what David requested; she had all but guaranteed a case of indigestion by eating two large slabs of David's favorite "kitchen-sink" pizza; she had heard his children's complaints about their first day of school. The evening was still early—she would stay a few more minutes to be polite, then leave.

While she waited for David to return, Toni examined the condo's living area more closely. The unit had come with average quality furnishings in reasonably good shape, to which David had added a few personal touches. A large calendar hung on the wall above the telephone; most of the squares for the current month were still empty. A business card was clipped to one edge. Something to do with that business David talked about buying into, maybe.

Above a table in the foyer hung a picture Toni had not seen before, and she walked over to look at it. The slightly enlarged photograph showed a pretty young woman in a full-skirted party dress. Toni guessed at the faded signature at the lower right-hand corner even before she leaned closer to read it: *Yours always, Jean.*

Mandy will resemble her mother more when she gets older. She will be a beautiful young woman someday.

From Josh's room the sound of lively music became louder when David opened the door, then faded again when he closed it behind him and returned to the living room. Mandy's door was also closed; for all practical purposes, Toni and David were alone.

Toni shivered when the sleeve of David's shirt brushed her bare arm, but he was apparently too absorbed in looking at the picture to notice.

"Your wife was a beautiful woman. Mandy is going to look a lot like her in a few years."

David seemed almost surprised. "I think she looks more like Jean's mother, Alice. Jean wanted the children to have this picture to remind them of what she looked like before she got sick—especially Josh. He was too small to remember her when she was well."

Toni felt tears forming from the knowledge that Jean Trent had not lived to see her daughter enter the seventh grade and her baby boy become a first grader.

"I know losing their mother has been very hard for them. They shouldn't ever lose her memory."

"Thank you for being here tonight." Once again, Toni felt David must have read her heart, and she felt ashamed that she had almost refused to come.

Toni turned from the picture to look at David. "Your children are very special to me. If there is ever anything I can do for them, I want you to let me know."

David's voice was husky. "You don't know how much that means, Toni. I realize I'm not much good as a father. I'm trying to learn, but there are some things I can't handle by myself. Mandy's at an age where she needs a woman to talk to."

Toni smiled wryly. "I know all about that. When I was her age, my life was a mess, and it continued that way until April and Evelyn took me in tow. I didn't trust anyone, and I sure didn't want to be told what to do. Looking back, it's a wonder I lived through it."

David regarded her tenderly, and Toni felt a moment of panic when she suspected he might kiss her. "I'm glad you survived, and so are the kids," he said. "You help us all just by caring."

Toni sought the right words to tell David not to expect more from her than she intended to give. She attempted to speak lightly. "I suppose that's the social worker coming out in me. Evelyn always believed that an ounce of prevention was worth a pound of cure when it comes to dealing with children, and in my line of work I've seen the truth of that statement many times."

"Nothing personal," he said, almost making it a question.

Toni lifted her chin and looked him in the eye. "I can't afford to make it personal."

A muscle worked in his jaw, but otherwise David's expression was impassive. "I understand."

Realizing she had been holding her breath, Toni exhaled deeply. "Thanks for dinner. I have some reports to review, so I'll be going now."

David walked with Toni to her SUV and waved as she

drove away into the deepening August twilight.

On her way home, Toni reviewed their conversation. Did David really understand she would not allow their association to become personal?

And more importantly, would she be able to keep it that way?

seventeen

After Toni got home from David's condo, she tried to work on a critical report due in Montgomery the following day, but she found it hard to concentrate and soon gave up. Her mind kept reviewing the strange way David had looked when she tried to tell him there would be nothing personal between them. She wondered if what she took as his disappointment could actually have been an attempt to disguise his relief.

This is ridiculous—I can't let David Trent interfere with my work.

She would have to see him again fairly often, since she had promised Evelyn—and David—to help with Josh and Mandy. She was a family friend and nothing more. The sooner all concerned accepted that truth, the easier it would be for Toni to be with them.

When she reached the office Thursday morning, Toni asked Anna Hastings to hold her calls while she finished the report. She filed it before the deadline, leaving a backlog of other work to catch up on.

Evelyn warned me it would be like this, Toni recalled early Friday when an emergency foster care situation promised to take up much of the day. It turned out to be the kind of day when everything that could go wrong, did. As a result, she was physically and emotionally exhausted when she left the DHR office late Friday afternoon.

As soon as she got home, Toni soaked away the day's tensions in a leisurely bubble bath. She had no commitments for the weekend and no plans to go anywhere except church on Sunday. She had made no plans to see David or the children, which was just as well. As much as she enjoyed his company, she and David had no future together, and the more she saw him, the harder it could become to remember that.

&

Although Toni kept thinking David might call, her telephone remained silent Friday night. Rain started early Saturday morning, making bicycle riding impossible. By Sunday morning, Toni fully expected David to bring the children to Community Church again and invite her to eat with them afterward. Like Evelyn, she wanted to see the children in Bible study, and she believed David would also benefit from it. But that did not mean she had to go anywhere with them afterward.

When she arrived at church on Sunday morning, Toni looked in vain for David's truck in the parking lot. Seeing Mark Elliott, the educational director, she asked if he had seen the Trents.

"Not today. Jeff told me he and Josh are in the same first grade classroom. I hope Josh will join Jeff's Bible study class as well."

"So do I."

Toni was disappointed that the children had not come to Bible study, but she still hoped David would bring them to the worship service. From the choir loft, Toni could view the entire sanctuary. If David and the children were there, she would see them.

The service began, the choir sang, and the announcements were made before Toni acknowledged that last Sunday's visitors were not going to make an appearance at Community Church on this day.

The realization grew into a sense of guilt. *I was so concerned David might ask me out, it never occurred to me to make sure his children came to church. If I had offered to pick up Josh and Mandy, they probably would have come. It's wrong of me to allow my vow not to become romantically involved with David keep me from helping his children.*

When the pastor opened a session of silent prayer, Toni raised her own earnest petition.

Lord, You know I haven't been the faithful witness I could have been. Lead me in the right direction and show me how to deal with Josh and Mandy and their father. Let them find the joy and comfort of Your love and may they know Your healing peace.

When Pastor Hurley said "Amen," Toni added her own "so be it." She had no doubt her prayer had been heard, but she also knew she had to do her part in its answer.

Even if it meant seeing more of David Trent than she would prefer.

❧

After the worship service, Toni was hanging up her choir robe when Janet Brown engaged her in conversation.

"We were hoping to see Evelyn Trent's brother today," Janet said.

So was I. "Apparently he and the children couldn't make it."

"Ted thinks David Trent looks like a baritone. Does he sing?"

"I have no idea."

Janet smiled. "From what I hear, you must be getting to know that family pretty well. I'm glad."

"As you know, Evelyn asked me to help the children as a sort of substitute aunt."

Janet seemed amused. "What does that make their father?"

"A friend," Toni said. "That's all."

"For now, maybe," Janet said. "Come home with us. Ted plans to grill a few hamburgers."

And you will no doubt grill me about the Trents. "Thanks, but not today."

"Tell David we hope to see him next Sunday."

"If I see him," Toni said pointedly.

"Oh, I imagine you'll see each other before then."

"Don't count on it. Despite what some people in this town seem to think, we're not a couple."

Janet grinned. "I'll see you at choir practice."

❧

Toni went home to a lunch of leftovers, still irritated at Janet's presumption about her relationship with David. Toni did not want to appear to be pursuing him, but she felt an obligation to find out the reason for the family's absence from church.

Maybe one of the children is ill and that's why they didn't come. After what I said the other night, David might not even let me know.

Toni dialed David's number and got a busy signal. *Maybe he's trying to get in touch with a doctor. I'll wait a few more minutes and try again, and if the line is still busy, I'll go over there and see what's happening.*

A few restless minutes later, Toni had her hand on the telephone to try the call again when it rang, startling her.

She picked up the receiver, and although Toni expected David to be the caller, she answered in her most professional manner. "Schmidt residence," she said crisply.

The familiar female voice at the other end sounded a long way off. "Hello, Toni. I wasn't sure you'd be at home this afternoon."

"Evelyn! I can hardly hear you. Where are you?"

"At the cruise line dock in Miami—we just came in and the place is a madhouse."

"How was your cruise?"

"Most enjoyable, but we can talk about that later. Tell me how you and the DHR office are getting along. Any problems?"

Toni briefed Evelyn about her work, concluding with the information that her first state reports had been filed on time.

"And thank you for the gift. The desk nameplate is beautiful. It almost makes me feel like I really belong there."

"That was my intention. I ordered it over the telephone and didn't get to see the finished product, but David said they did a good job and you liked it."

"When did you talk to him?" asked Toni.

"Just now. I was glad to hear you went biking with him and the children. They spend far too much time indoors. I hope you can go riding with them regularly."

"I will when the weather cooperates. It rained yesterday, and of course the children have started school now, so they won't have as much free time."

"From what they told me, Josh and Mandy don't like school very much."

"They've been going only three days, and Rockdale is still a bit like a foreign country. With a little more time, I'm sure they'll adjust to living here."

"I hope so. It'll help if you keep urging them to go to church."

Toni wondered exactly what David had told his sister. "I intend to."

"Good. They'll listen to you, and so will David. What about the house? Are you having any problems with it?"

"Everything is fine. Don't worry about us."

Static crackled on the line, followed by the distorted sound of a loudspeaker in the background. "I must go now—I'll call again when I get to California. It means a great deal to me to know you're there for Josh and Mandy—and for my brother. I'm proud of you, Toni. Keep up the good work."

Toni replaced the receiver and sighed. Evelyn obviously took it for granted that her involvement, not only with David's children, but also with their father, would continue. Evelyn might no longer be there in person, but in a way, she was still playing the role of matchmaker.

All right, Evelyn. I intend to help the children as much as they'll let me, and I'll do what I can to keep them coming to Bible study. But don't expect me to fall into their father's arms in the process.

Toni had just picked up the newspaper when the telephone rang again. *That must be David, wanting to talk about Evelyn's call,* Toni guessed.

"Hi, Toni, it's Mary. Have you got a minute?"

"Sure. How are you holding up after the wear and tear of the first days of school?"

"I took a nap after church. The first few weeks are always hard—and this year's class could be quite a challenge."

Toni was beginning to suspect the reason for Mary's call. "Is Josh Trent part of that challenge?"

"Unfortunately, yes. As you know, he's a darling little boy and quite intelligent."

"I also know he's a whiner who can't tie his own shoes," Toni said.

Mary laughed. "I see a lot of those in my line of work. That's not his main problem, though."

Toni felt uneasy. She didn't like the drift of the conversation and wondered if they were betraying both Josh and David by having it. "Have you spoken to his father?"

"Not yet. I won't tell David Trent I talked to you, but I thought you should know that Josh is telling everyone he's getting a new mommy soon. Friday, Eddie Moore accused him of lying, and Josh became so angry I had to separate them."

Toni feared the worst. "Did Josh name this supposed new mommy?"

"No, but who else could it be but you?"

"His imagination, I suspect. Josh told me he wants to go back to Virginia and live with his grandmother again."

"Yes, he likes to talk about all the fun things he did in Virginia. It could be that seeing everyone else with their mothers on the first day of school triggered a bit of wishful thinking. I wanted your input before I talked to his father."

"What will you tell David?"

"The same thing I told you, but mostly that Josh needs to learn how to control his anger before it gets him into serious trouble."

Even though she knew Mary's assessment was fair, Toni rose to Josh's defense. "His family has been through a lot in the past couple of years. I really don't know how much more David can do for the boy."

"Other than helping him with anger management. . . ," Mary paused, then spoke lightly, "he can get Josh a new mommy. I could mention a certain social worker as an ideal candidate."

"No, thanks. Short of that, I do want to help Josh. He's

been to a Bible study class at Community once, and now that he's in first grade with Jeff Elliott, I hope he'll want to go every Sunday."

"Good. If Evelyn had stayed here, she would probably have brought the children to First Church. It's better for both of us for Josh not to be in my Sunday school department. No child should have to face the same teacher six days a week."

"I hadn't thought of that, but it makes sense. When will you talk to David?"

"Today, I hope. I'm calling all my students' parents to set up a home visit, but I never discuss behavior problems in front of the children."

"I know you make those visits on your own time—anyone who thinks teachers are overpaid doesn't know many like you."

"I could say the same about social workers. People don't go into our types of work for the money."

"They shouldn't, anyway. Do me a favor—if Josh gets into any more trouble, will you let me know?"

"You're listed as the emergency contact if David can't be reached, but if anything serious happens—which I don't anticipate—I'll let you know."

"Thanks. When you have time for us to get together again, give me a call."

"I will. And one more thing. . ." Mary paused.

"What?" Toni prompted.

"Don't be too hard on Josh's dad. He needs you too."

Mary hung up before Toni had a chance to reply, which was just as well. *What makes Mary think I'm being hard on David? I want to help his children, but despite what everyone in Rockdale seems to believe, I'm not pursuing David Trent.*

Toni returned to her newspaper, but when she found herself rereading the same paragraph several times, she put the paper down and went to sit on the front porch. She would have to talk to David eventually, but she would give Mary time to call him first.

Even as Toni rehearsed what she should say to David, she

heard him call her name. Surprised, she saw David and the children riding their bicycles on the sidewalk in front of the house.

"Get your bike and come with us," David invited.

Toni remained in the swing with her arms crossed. "That sounds a lot like an order." *And you know by now I don't take orders well.*

He looked contrite. "I meant it as an invitation."

Toni looked at Mandy, who was obviously less than thrilled to be there. "Where are you going?"

"To some park with a playground. Daddy says there's one around here somewhere."

"The only one I know about is on Jackson Street, on the other side of your condo. You've already come several blocks out of your way."

"Daddy said you'd go with us if we came and got you," said Josh.

Toni spoke directly to Josh. "I didn't see you at church this morning. Jeff's daddy said your friend hoped you'd be at Bible study."

"We didn't go 'cause Mandy couldn't go," Josh said.

Toni shifted her attention to Mandy. "Why not?"

"I didn't feel good."

"Mandy calls me a baby, but she's the one always cryin'," Josh said.

Toni looked at David for verification. *I'm sorry,* his expression said.

"I wanna go to the playground. Please come with us, Toni." Josh spoke emphatically but without whining.

"All right, since you asked nicely. I'll get my helmet and bike."

When they reached the playground some ten minutes later, David and Toni sat at a shady picnic table and watched Josh run toward the swings. "Push me," he demanded of Mandy, and to Toni's surprise, she did so without complaint.

"Something must be wrong with Mandy," Toni said. She spoke ironically, but David took her seriously.

"I'm afraid so. I've caught her crying several times since school started, and this morning she literally cried herself sick."

"I take it she still doesn't like Rockdale Middle School."

"That's putting it mildly. She keeps comparing it to her last school, and I have a feeling if anyone tried to be friendly, she'd shoot them down."

"It'll get better with time. At her age, girls tend to cry at the drop of a hat."

"I hope that's all it is."

Toni saw an opening and took it. "What about Josh? How is he doing?"

David's expression told Toni he had heard from Mary Oliver. "Josh doesn't cry—he just gets into fights. So far, I'm batting zero on my theory we'd feel like a family again once we came to Rockdale."

"Don't be so hard on yourself—or them. They're good kids, and they'll come around, probably sooner than later."

David reached for Toni's hand and held it loosely. "You know, I really misjudged you."

"How?"

His blue eyes held her gaze. "At first I believed you didn't like my children. Now I see you handle them better than I do. You couldn't do that if you didn't feel something for them."

"I am fond of Josh and Mandy, but don't put yourself down. You're learning together, and you love each other. That goes a long way."

"I still need a lot of help. I'd like to know that you'll set me straight when I need it and be there for the kids when I can't be." David searched Toni's face as if to gauge her reaction. "I know that's a big imposition," he added.

"I don't consider helping Josh and Mandy an imposition. In a way, I suppose you could say I'm taking Evelyn's place with them, just as I took her place at DHR."

David released her hand and rubbed his chin. "I suppose Evelyn called you—she said she was going to."

Toni nodded. "I assured her everything was all right here."

"She asked me to take care of you. I told her it seems you're doing all the caretaking so far."

Toni raised her chin. "Evelyn knows I'm used to being on my own. If I need help, I'll ask for it."

David smiled. "I won't hold my breath waiting for that."

"Good. You might turn very blue. While we're on the subject, Evelyn asked me to do something else."

"If you're talking about getting them into Bible study at Community, I told her I would."

"Even if Mandy cries and doesn't want to go?"

David sighed. "Yes, Toni, even then. I know I should have put my foot down this morning, but I felt so sorry for her I just couldn't."

"Don't worry about it, but I think you'll find the rest of the week goes better after you've been in God's house. It always works that way for me."

"That's a good thing—otherwise, I doubt you could put up with the likes of us."

Josh came running back then, as eager to leave the playground as he had been to get there. "It's hot. I want to go home."

"Try that again without the whiny voice," David said. When he did, David and Toni applauded, and for once Mandy had nothing sarcastic to add.

This might be a good time for me to try to talk to her. The thought grew, and when the children reached the condo ahead of them and went inside to cool off, she decided to act upon it.

"If you don't mind, I'd like to borrow Mandy for a few hours."

David looked surprised. "What for?"

"I want to show her something. We can ride to my house and I'll bring her and her bike home."

"I'll tell her," David said. *I don't know what you're up to, but I think it will be good,* his expression said.

I'm not sure myself, but I have to try, Toni answered silently.

eighteen

It was just past four o'clock when Toni and Mandy reached Evelyn's house. Mandy had readily agreed to come along, even though Toni had not specified where they were going. Josh had also wanted to go, and David had to promise to take him somewhere special too.

"Leave your bike in the garage beside mine. We'll take the SUV," Toni directed.

"I'm glad you didn't let Josh come with us," Mandy said when they pulled away from the curb. "He's such a baby."

"Josh has a lot of growing up to do," Toni said.

"I suppose you think I do too," Mandy said. "I'll be glad when I am grown up and people quit telling me how to act and what to do all the time."

Toni laughed. "I remember saying something like that to my friend April once. She told me no one has ever lived that long." Then seeing the hurt in Mandy's eyes, Toni added, "I know what you mean, though, because I felt that way myself when I was your age."

I doubt it, Mandy's expression said. "Where are we going?"

"Down memory lane, you might say. Like you, I was twelve when I came to Rockdale. I haven't been back to the first place where I lived in many years."

"I never saw this part of town before," Mandy said when Toni turned down a pothole-pocked street lined with ramshackle, unpainted houses. Rusting appliances and automobile bodies dotted many of the untended, weed-choked yards. "I suppose it looked a lot better then," she added diplomatically.

"Not much." Toni slowed before a shotgun house at the end of the street. Its boarded windows and sagging roof testified the house had been abandoned. "I lived here for several months."

Mandy's wrinkled her nose in distaste. "Where did you go to school back then?"

Back then—to Mandy, any time before she was born is ancient history. "Nowhere, for a long time. It was spring when we moved here, and we stayed through the summer and moved again when. . ." Toni stopped herself. Mandy didn't need to hear all the sordid details. "When we found another place."

"Who's 'we'? Who was in your family?"

I didn't have a family, Toni could have said. "At that time, it was my stepmother and my father. He drove a truck and didn't come home very often."

"So you had a stepmother?"

Toni nodded. "Several, as a matter of fact."

Mandy was silent for a moment. "When Daddy marries again, Josh and I will have a stepmother."

Not "if" but "when." *It's obvious Mandy has been thinking about a "new mommy" too.* Not wanting to comment on that subject, Toni pointed out the roads leading to Community Church and Warren Mountain as they passed them.

"I'd like to ride my bike all the way up that mountain without Josh this fall."

"Some of the girls in your class would probably go with you if you asked them," Toni said.

"Or not," Mandy said.

"You'll never know until you try."

Mandy remained silent until they passed a battered metal sign obviously used for target practice. "Now leaving Rockdale," she read out loud.

"That's a very old city limits sign. I don't know why it's still there. As you can see, we aren't really out of town at all."

Toni pulled into an aging mobile home park. "This is the next place I lived."

"It doesn't look much better." Mandy blurted out the words, then looked embarrassed.

"It wasn't," Toni said. "There's the lot—the one with the big tree stump in front. Of course, that's not the same house trailer. I'm sure the one I lived in was junked years ago. It wasn't in very good shape to begin with."

"Did you have a bike then?"

Toni blinked at Mandy's non sequitur. "No. April Kincaid gave me my first bicycle."

"Were you living here then?"

"No. I'll show you the last place I stayed before I went to your aunt Evelyn's house."

Mandy remained silent as Toni left the mobile home park and drove back to the center of town. Circling the courthouse, she drove south to Potter Road, on the outskirts of town.

"The Potters were my foster parents," Toni said. "They had several children of their own and also took in strays like me." Toni slowed, then stopped in front of a large, white farmhouse that had seen better days.

"The mailbox says R. Johnson. The Potters must not live here anymore," Mandy said.

"That's right. They left town before I did," Toni said.

"It doesn't look like such a bad house," Mandy said cautiously.

"It was all right, but it never felt like a real home to me. The Potters had several young children, and I looked after them. I didn't mind, though, since I never had any real brothers or sisters."

Mandy was silent for a moment. "Aunt Evelyn never said anything about where all you'd lived."

"There was no reason for her to." Now that Toni had Mandy's attention, she spoke earnestly. "God has led me on an amazing journey. From the time I was your age until April Kincaid came into my life, I got into a lot of trouble. I ran away several times. I broke into April's apartment to steal a blanket because I had been sleeping outside and I was cold. I believe God sent me there because He knew I needed a friend. With His help and the help of April and your aunt, I turned my life around." Toni stopped, overcome by unexpected emotion.

Mandy spoke quietly. "Does Daddy know about all of that?"

"He hasn't seen the places where I lived—but he knows how I lived before his sister took me in."

"Daddy likes you a lot," Mandy said matter-of-factly.

What can I say to that? Help me, Lord.

"I like all of you a lot too, and I want you to be happy living here."

Mandy began to cry, her tears running unchecked down her cheeks. "It's been so hard. . . ."

Toni lifted the center console and handed Mandy a tissue from the box she kept there for such situations. "I know, Mandy. But God knew what He was doing when He brought you here, and He'll help you through anything if you ask Him."

Mandy dabbed at her eyes. "I asked God to make my mother well, but she kept getting sicker, then she died. I don't think God listens to me."

"I've felt that way myself, many times. We don't understand God's ways, but Proverbs 3:6 tells us, 'In all thy ways acknowledge Him, and He shall direct thy paths.' "

"I never heard that before," Mandy said.

"I hadn't heard it when I was twelve, either. I remember I was surprised to find the Bible has so much practical advice in it."

Toni's cell phone rang, and she looked at the caller ID feature and sighed. "It's the police chief," she told Mandy.

After a brief conversation with Earl Hurley, Toni turned to Mandy. "I'm sorry, but I must make an emergency placement. I'll have to take you home now." Toni put away the cell phone and headed the SUV back toward town.

"What's an emergency placement?"

"When a child needs to be removed from a dangerous or harmful situation right away, DHR is notified. In this case, both parents have been arrested on drug charges and there's no one to take care of their two-year-old daughter."

"I want to go with you," said Mandy.

"First I'm going home to call around until I find a foster parent who can take the child. Then I'll pick her up and make the transfer."

"What if nobody can take her?" Mandy asked.

"Do you remember seeing the crib in your aunt Evelyn's spare room? That's why it's there."

"I didn't know you had to do that," Mandy said.

"Fortunately, it seldom happens, but that's part of my job."

Toni stopped in front of her house, and Mandy got out.

"You don't have to take me home. I can ride my bike."

"Thanks. I do need to start calling right away. I'm sorry we didn't have more time to visit."

"So am I."

Toni opened her arms, and Mandy came into them and hugged her warmly.

"Thank you, Toni."

Thank You, Lord, for showing me what to say to Mandy. Now help me find a home for this other little girl.

❧

Toni was halfway down her calling list before she found a foster parent willing to take on a two-year-old child, even temporarily. By the time she had picked up the little girl at the police station and settled her in the foster home, it was well past supper time. She did not feel particularly hungry, but Toni picked up a fast-food sandwich on her way home.

The day had been exhausting, but Toni's sense of accomplishment more than compensated for her fatigue. Seeing the answering machine's message light flashing in the dark, she hoped it wouldn't be another emergency call.

"Call me when you get in," David's voice ordered.

What does he want now? Something in the tone of his voice made her uneasy, and she called him back immediately.

"Toni—I was worried about you. Is everything all right?"

"Of course—why wouldn't it be?"

"Mandy told me you had an emergency. I think she was a little spooked."

"I don't know why. Tell Mandy everything went well. It was a routine emergency placement."

David sounded less tense. "If an emergency can be routine. Anyway, thanks for spending time with Mandy."

"What did she say about it?"

"Not much—she mentioned you took her to some places where you used to live."

"I intended to take her to supper too—maybe next time we won't be interrupted."

"She knows it wasn't your fault."

Toni suppressed a yawn. "That's good."

"I won't keep you any longer—you sound tired."

"Thanks for your concern. Tell Mandy I enjoyed her company."

"I think it was mutual. Good-bye, Toni. I'll see you soon."

❧

Toni spent most of Monday working on the necessary legal procedures to turn the previous day's emergency placement into a more permanent arrangement. She went to the jail to interview the parents to make sure there were no family members who could take custody of their daughter and asked Judge Oliver to expedite the hearing giving DHR the power to act in the child's best interests. Finally, Toni checked the regular list of foster parents and found a couple who had just lost a foster child to adoption—a happy result not seen often enough in the foster care system.

Toni came home Monday night pleased with the way her first emergency had turned out. Since Mandy had seemed so interested, Toni called to give her a report.

"How long will the little girl be away from her parents?" Mandy asked.

"That's hard to say. Their case has to go through the courts. There will be a trial, and if they're acquitted and want her back, we'll decide what to do then. If they go to jail, DHR will look after the child until the parents are released and can prove they can provide a good, safe home for her."

"Poor little girl," Mandy said. "I hope the people she's with will be good to her."

"We check our foster homes regularly—she'll be fine."

"Thanks for letting me know. Oh, Daddy says he wants to talk to you," Mandy said when Toni was about to hang up.

David sounded about as excited as she had ever heard him. "You won't believe this, but I just found a perfect baby-sitter living right next door." Toni's image of a gum-chewing teenager faded quickly when David told her Mrs. Tarpley was a widow and had recently retired. "She was away visiting one of her children when we moved in, but she came over with a plate of cookies this afternoon. She's agreed to stay with the kids after school tomorrow."

"What's happening then?"

"I'll be tied up with some business. I wanted to let you know Mrs. Tarpley would be here."

"I'll come by and check on them after work, just in case," Toni said.

"They'd like that—and you can meet Mrs. Tarpley. I think you'll like her."

"Your neighbor sounds like an answer to prayer."

"You really mean that, don't you?"

"I pray for you and the children every day. I believe Mrs. Tarpley is there because you need her."

"I hadn't thought of that, but I suppose it's possible. Keep praying. We need all the help we can get."

"You can pray too, you know," Toni reminded him.

"What makes you think I don't?"

Toni heard Mandy's voice in the background, and David turned away from the telephone. "I'll be right there," she heard him say, then he came back on the line. "Sorry, but Mandy needs help her with math."

"Give Mrs. Tarpley my work, home, and cell phone numbers and tell her to call me if she needs anything."

"She will. You're first on the list of emergency numbers. Good-bye, Toni—and thanks."

Toni continued holding the receiver even after David broke the connection. *Thanks for praying for them?*

Every time Toni thought she was beginning to understand David Trent, he managed to do something else to show how much she still had to learn about him. If he wanted to accept her as a family friend and emergency contact, that was fine.

She wanted nothing more.

ॐ

The children seemed genuinely glad to see Toni after work on Tuesday. Mrs. Tarpley was a calm, country-bred woman whose sharp eyes missed nothing; the children would not be likely to get away with anything when she was there. *Just what they need,* Toni thought and once again thanked God the woman had come their way.

After Mandy asked Toni what kind of schoolwork she had done that day, she showed her a project she and another girl were doing for their social studies class. "We're going to work on it at her house after school tomorrow," Mandy said.

"That's one way to make friends," Toni said.

"I know everyone in my class," Josh said. He proudly displayed a primary pad on which his first name was printed in crooked letters.

"Won't you stay for supper?" Mrs. Tarpley invited when Toni started to leave. "I cooked us a pot roast, and there's aplenty."

Toni was tempted to accept, but she did not want to be there when David came home. "Thank you, but I must be going." At the door, she paused and looked from Josh to Mandy. "Whose turn is it to say grace tonight?"

"Mine!" exclaimed Josh.

"No, it's not—you said it last time."

"You can both say a blessing, then," Toni suggested.

Mrs. Tarpley laughed. "I can think of worse things for them to be arguin' about."

"So can I," Toni agreed.

Toni felt reassured by her visit. The children seemed to be getting along better with each other and at school, and they were doing their homework. She had told David things would be better; perhaps they were already turning in that direction.

ૐ

On Wednesday, Toni had been reviewing case files all morning without a break when Anna Hastings knocked on her office door.

"Lunchtime."

Toni looked up in surprise. "Already? It can't be."

"It's nearly noon."

Toni glanced at her watch. "So it is, but I want to do a few more files. If you're going out, would you bring me back a sandwich?"

"There's a caller here with a different idea," Anna said.

"A caller?"

"A gentleman caller," Anna emphasized.

Toni reluctantly left her office. That David Trent waited in the reception area was no surprise; he was the only man in Rockdale likely to expect Toni to drop everything to have lunch with him.

David smiled engagingly. "I know you're busy, but you still need to eat. Let's go to lunch."

"I really don't have time," Toni said.

"We can grab a quick sandwich. I have something to show you."

"What is it?"

"I can't tell you—you have to see it for yourself."

Toni wavered, then capitulated when her curiosity won out. "All right, but it had better not take long."

After telling Anna she would be back in thirty minutes, Toni followed David into the oppressive midday heat of late August. The leather seats in his truck were hot to the touch, and the blast from the air conditioner felt more like a blast furnace.

"I don't know why I let you talk me into this," Toni said.

He smiled. "It must be because of my great charm."

"Or my idiocy."

When he stopped in the Loading Zone Only space in

front of Statum's Family Restaurant, Toni's heart sank. If she and David were seen together again, Toni could imagine what the Rockdale rumor mill would grind out. *Have you heard? Evelyn Trent's good-looking brother is courting Toni Schmidt. Why, every time you see one, there's the other.*

Again, David seemed to anticipate Toni's reaction. "Stay here. I'll leave the motor running so you'll have the air conditioning. I won't be gone long."

Toni tried to sink out of sight in the seat, but Jenny Suiter spotted her and did a double take. She waved at Toni and went inside the restaurant. *Where she will see David and speculate why I'm sitting here in his truck when I ought to be in the office, tending to DHR business.*

"I must be getting paranoid," Toni said aloud. As long as she knew she was in the right, what others might say had never concerned her. However, gossip about her and David was both different and unwelcome.

David returned in a few minutes, a Statum's takeout bag in one hand and two containers of lemonade in the other.

"Where are we going?" she asked when he pulled away from the curb.

"You'll see."

David made a right turn, then another, bringing them to a parking lot almost directly behind Statum's Restaurant. He pulled into a shady space and turned off the engine. "Here we are."

"We're having lunch in a parking lot?"

"No." David came around the truck and opened her door. "Your balance is better than mine—you can carry the drinks. We're going over there."

Toni followed him across the parking lot to the side entrance of a one-story brick office building. David unlocked the door and motioned for her to enter.

Toni looked around the room, which was about the size of her DHR office. The furnishings, a haphazard collection of styles and materials, consisted of a large desk with a swivel chair, two side chairs, a filing cabinet, and a long table on which several stacks of papers awaited stapling. A plastic tablecloth set with paper plates and disposable cutlery covered the desk.

"Where am I?" she asked.

David laughed. "Certainly not in Kansas."

Toni pointed to another door to the right of the filing cabinet. "Is the Emerald City of Oz on the other side?"

"Look and see."

Aware that David watched in amusement, Toni opened the door onto a much larger, mostly unfurnished room. Its only occupant, a man in coveralls, stood with his back to them, carefully adding another name to the one already on the large front window.

Toni read the backward letters of the top name: N O S N E B. "This is the Benson Insurance Agency?"

"It was. Fred Benson Senior died last year. I heard his son needed a partner, and we were able to work out a deal."

Why didn't you tell me about this? The question was on her lips before Toni realized it was not her concern. "I had no idea," she said instead.

David looked pleased. "I knew as soon as my name went on the window everyone in town would see it, but I wanted you to be the first to know."

Toni looked around the office, mentally calculating the amount of work ahead to bring the agency back to life. "Congratulations, I think."

"Thanks, I think. I'll tell you about it while we eat—I know you have work to do."

"Does Evelyn know about this?" Toni asked when David had filled in the details.

"She knew I was negotiating with someone, but I asked her to keep it quiet until we closed the deal, which we did yesterday."

"What do you know about the insurance business?"

"Enough. Jean's stepfather has an agency in Virginia, and I lived there long enough to learn the ropes. I'll have to take a few courses and pass a test, but Freddy Benson will do the paperwork until I have my license."

"I suppose this means you're in Rockdale to stay."

David smiled wryly. "After paying what all this will cost, the only other place I can afford is the poorhouse."

"Which is where I could end up if I don't get back to work."

⌘

"Thanks for your time," David said when he pulled into the DHR parking lot.

"Thanks for the lunch—it seems you're always feeding me." She felt as if "I don't know how to deal with all this attention" was written all over her face.

"It's no big deal." His gaze seemed to respond, *When will you realize that I like being with you?*

Toni hurried back to her desk, aware not only that her promised thirty-minute absence had lasted far longer, but that Anna and Edwinna had no doubt been discussing her involvement with David Trent. Telling them the truth might not stop their speculations, but Toni decided it was her best defense.

"David Trent has bought into the Benson Insurance Agency, and we had sandwiches in his new office. If Judge Oliver calls, tell him I have some papers he needs to sign."

Back in her office, Toni stared blindly at the file before her, wishing her mind and her heart could agree about David Trent. She didn't know whether to feel dismayed or flattered that David wanted her to be the first to see his new office. It implied a closeness she had not sought and did not want.

Toni had vowed they could have no future together, but the more she saw him, the harder it would be to remain his friend.

nineteen

The moment Toni arrived at choir practice on Thursday evening, Janet Brown greeted her with the latest rumor.

"Word is you and David Trent were seen in the parking lot behind Statum's Restaurant yesterday. What was that all about?"

"Nothing worth mentioning. David has bought an interest in the Benson Insurance Agency, and he was showing me the office."

Janet nodded knowingly. "That sounds as if you two are getting to be something more than friends."

"Don't believe everything you hear. You know I have no romantic interest in David Trent—or anyone else."

Janet sounded doubtful. "Are you sure about that?"

"He's a good man, and I promised Evelyn to help with his children. I consider us to be friends—and that's all."

Ted Brown had been listening to their conversation and now joined it. "From what Mark Elliott says, David Trent is looking for more than a friend."

"What makes him say that?" asked Janet.

"Josh Trent is in Jeff Elliott's first grade class. He told Jeff he was getting a new mommy real soon—any day now."

Toni groaned inwardly. *Not that "new mommy" business again!*

"Josh said something like that the first day of school, but I doubt anyone took him seriously."

"Jeff apparently did, but he said some of the other children laughed at Josh and said he should stop telling such stories."

Unaware Josh was still repeating the new mommy story, Toni tried to downplay it while concealing her own concern. "You know how children tend to exaggerate. This story seems to have taken off on its own."

"This is one story I'd like to turn out to be true," Janet said.

"You would make a great new mommy for Josh."

Toni made no effort to hide her irritation. "I'm not about to be, and I would appreciate it very much if you both would make that clear to anyone who brings it up."

Janet sighed. "All right, but you shouldn't close your mind to the possibility."

"Places, everyone," Ted called out. "We have a great anthem to rehearse tonight, so let's get started."

"Good," Toni muttered. She had heard more than enough talk about Josh's new mommy for one day.

&

On her way home, Toni decided David should know the extent to which Josh's original "new mommy" story was being spread. His father should also Josh was still being teased about it.

When she went to the telephone to call him, Toni saw the answering machine light blinking. David. What does he want?

His message was terse. "Call back when you get home."

There was an edge in David's voice Toni had seldom heard, and her first thought was that something had happened to one of the children. Toni called him back immediately, and he picked up the telephone on the first ring.

"I'm coming over," he said with his usual directness.

"Is something wrong?"

David hung up without replying, so Toni went outside to wait in the porch swing. When David's truck pulled up to the curb, she saw he was alone. Even in the dim glow of the corner streetlight, David looked troubled.

He ran up the walkway and took the porch steps in several strides. "Let's go inside."

Toni closed the front door behind them and turned to face David. "Where are the children? Are they all right?"

"What? Oh, yes. They're both in bed, and Mrs. Tarpley's there."

Toni pointed to the couch. "Sit down. Can I get you

something? I have lemonade in the refrigerator."

"No, thanks." David sat on the edge of the couch. "I don't know what I'm going to do about Josh. He got into a fight on the school playground at recess this morning and had to sit in the principal's office the rest of the day. Mary Oliver said if it happens again, Josh could be expelled."

Toni put her hand to her throat. "I can't believe the school would do that to Josh. What was the fight about?"

"It goes back to something Josh said on the first day of school. I suspect the other kids in his class have been egging him on to keep the story going."

Although Toni thought she already knew the answer, she had to ask the question anyway. "What did Josh say that was bad enough to start a fight?"

"Do you remember how upset Josh was that first day when all the others in his class came with their mothers?"

Toni nodded. "Yes, but we talked about that. I thought Josh understood having his daddy with him made him special."

"Not special enough, apparently." David looked away from Toni. "Josh told everyone he was getting a new mommy of his own. Some of the children believed him, but others kept taunting him. Today he had enough of it and pushed one of the boys hard enough to knock him down. The child wasn't hurt, but Mary Oliver said he came close to hitting his head on a metal slide. He could have been seriously hurt."

"What does Josh have to say about what happened?"

"Not much. He doesn't seem to understand what all the fuss is about, since no one was hurt."

"Josh apparently told the same story at his Bible study class, except there he said he was getting this supposed new mommy right away."

David looked up, surprised. "Why didn't you tell me this before?"

"I just heard about it at choir practice tonight. I told the person who said it I didn't know where Josh got such an idea and said it isn't worth repeating."

David shook his head. "The damage had already been done, I'm afraid, and it's all my fault. There's something about this you don't know. I should have told you, but. . ."

Toni shivered under the intensity of David's gaze, and her heart beat faster as she waited for him to speak. "I'm listening," she prompted.

David's jaw muscle tightened. "This is hard to talk about. Bear with me, and I'll try to get through it."

He took a deep breath and glanced at Toni. "Jean wanted me to leave the army when Josh was born, but I was up for a big promotion, so I stayed in. I was overseas when Jean got sick, and I blame myself for not being there when she needed me. She worried more about the children than herself. The sicker she got, the more she worried about them. Her mother and stepfather loved the children, but they let them do more or less as they pleased. Everything just got worse. . . ." David paused for a moment, his eyes bright with unshed tears, and Toni's heart went out to him. When she put her hand in his, he grasped it and continued to speak.

"When I finally got leave to come back to the States, Jean was in the hospital. She'd been almost too weak to talk at first, but that day she seemed so much stronger I thought God had finally granted the miracle I had prayed for so long and so hard. She wanted to see the children, so I got permission to bring them in. I lifted Josh to sit in the bed on the side away from the IV tubes. Mandy and I stood on the other side. Mandy stroked her mother's cheek, and I held Jean's hand. She asked the children what they had been doing, and they talked to her for awhile. Then Jean told them she had something important to say and she wanted them to hear and remember it."

David stopped again, and Toni felt tears coming into her own eyes as she pictured the scene. She squeezed his hand in encouragement, and he took a deep breath and began to speak more rapidly. "Jean said—her exact words—'David, I
̶ you'll do your best to take care of our children, but you

can't do it alone. I want you to vow to me and to them to marry again and give them a new mother.' The children cried and told her they didn't want another mother, and I had to take them out of the room. I tried to tell them their mother would be all right, but that night, she went into a coma. Jean lived for several more weeks, but she never spoke again."

"Of course you made that vow."

David released Toni's hand to wipe his eyes. "Of course I did—what else could I do? I knew the children needed me, so I left the army as soon as I could."

Toni took a deep breath. David's story had changed her perception of several things. Evelyn had more in mind than romance for David. Toni could almost hear what Evelyn must have told him. *Toni lost her own mother at an early age. She knows what it's like, and she loves children. She would make Josh and Mandy a wonderful stepmother. . . .*

"So you came to Rockdale to find a mother for your children," Toni said flatly.

David shook his head. "I couldn't leave them with the Websters, and I couldn't think of a better place than Rockdale for us to put down new roots. I've never spoken of that day with the children, and I'm not sure Josh remembers it. I thought he told his classmates he was getting a new mommy because of what happened the first day of school."

David spoke so sincerely, so obviously from his heart, that Toni felt moved to respond the same way. "I wasn't going to tell you this, but I think Josh does remember. The first day I met the children, he asked me if I was his new mommy."

David stared at Toni. "I had no idea—what did you tell him?"

"I asked Josh if he wanted a new mommy, and he said no, he wanted his old mommy to come back from heaven. I acknowledged how much he must miss her, then I told him that heaven is a wonderful place and that she is happy there. That seemed to satisfy him."

"You always seem to know the right thing, while I. . ."

David broke off, despair mirrored on his face. "I want to be a good father, but I don't seem to know how. I don't know how to deal with my son."

Moved by his anguish, Toni put her hand on his arm. "Things aren't that bad. Mary Oliver can help us with Josh."

David looked surprised. "Did you say 'us'?"

"Us," she repeated. "I love Josh too, you know."

"Oh, Toni. . ."

David pulled Toni into his arms and hugged her almost breathless, then drew back slightly and touched her cheek with the back of his hand.

"I don't know how I would manage without you."

"Very well, I imagine." Toni's voice sounded strange in her ears, and she realized she was trembling.

"We both know better."

David drew her close again, and with her head against his chest, Toni heard the steady beating of his heart. He stroked her hair and traced the line of her chin, then he kissed her tenderly. In response, Toni put her arms around his neck and hugged him briefly before drawing back.

"Thanks," David said huskily.

Toni smiled. "For what?"

David stood. "For everything—for being you—for being here for me."

"And the children," she added.

David regarded Toni with the intent look she had never quite understood. "How willing are you to help Josh?"

"What?"

"If you want to help my son, make his story come true. Marry me."

Toni felt her world spinning out of control. "I can't."

David's face clouded. "Why?"

"There's something you should know about me too. Years before you vowed to marry again, I vowed never to marry at all."

"Evelyn told me about your vow and the reason behind it. But you must know I could never hurt you the way your father hurt your mother."

Toni stood and went to the front door. "I think you should go now."

David looked baffled. "I don't understand you, Toni."

"Sometimes, neither do I. Good night, David."

He lingered at the door. "If you change your mind. . ."

I won't. Toni almost voiced the words, but stopped. *Don't say anything you'll regret later,* something warned her.

"Good night, David," she repeated.

※

The next two days Toni vacillated between hoping David would call her and fearing he might. She reviewed all the times they had been together and everything that had happened between them from the beginning.

Toni admitted she had been falling in love with David all along, even though she'd denied it. Had he asked her to marry him in any other way or at another time, she might have given him a different answer. She loved his children and wanted the best for them, but she also knew it would not be fair to them or to her if their father married her only to give them a mother.

What should I have done that I didn't?

It was not a question Toni could answer on her own, and during her quiet time on Saturday, Toni reflected on the degree to which she had let God guide her decisions. When she prayed, Toni knew she had a tendency to ask for her own will to be done, rather than allowing the Holy Spirit to guide her. Tears filled her eyes as Toni recalled the many things she had stubbornly held on to, rather than turning them over to God.

On a day like this, rote prayers had no meaning. Toni sank to her knees and shared her heart with the only One whose help was always there.

"Lord, You know why I made that vow not to marry. You know how much I was hurt from all the bad things that happened to me."

Yes, Child. Give it all to me, and I will heal your heart.

"Lord, if You mean for me to be David's wife, even though

he doesn't love me, I will. And if the answer is no, grant me Your peace."

My peace you always have. My grace is sufficient. Trust me.

"I want to, Lord. Help me."

I will, my child.

twenty

Even though Toni had dismissed David's proposal of marriage, she realized he could never be out of her life as long as they both lived in Rockdale. In such a small town, avoiding David altogether was impossible, especially since she intended to maintain a relationship with his children. Not only would David and Josh and Mandy never be completely out of her sight, they would remain in her mind and heart. And at the moment, Toni was concerned about Josh.

Is he really in danger of being expelled, or is David overreacting? Toni glanced at her watch and decided it was not too late to call Mary Oliver.

Her friend answered on the first ring and did not seem surprised to receive Toni's call. "Hi, Toni. I suppose you heard what happened to Josh."

"Yes, but I thought we had an agreement that you'd let me know if Josh got into serious trouble."

"I would have, but the way things developed, I didn't have time. I knew you had choir practice that night, and I figured David Trent would tell you, anyway."

"He did, but from what David said, the child Josh hit wasn't hurt. I can't believe he's in danger of expulsion."

"Unfortunately, he is. The Rockdale school board adopted a zero tolerance policy a couple of years ago. Teachers are expected to enforce each part of every rule, no matter the circumstances. It doesn't help that the boy Josh knocked down is Cody Marshall, a nephew of the school board president. Sam Marshall called me at home that night to say if Josh so much as touches another child, out he goes."

"David is really upset about this. He had talked to Josh about controlling his temper and thought everything would be all right, but apparently when someone pushes Josh, he pushes back."

"Shoves back is more like it. I don't have any magic solution, but Josh might listen to you. In case you didn't know it, the little guy is quite attached to you."

"I suppose I can try," Toni said.

"One more thing—I hear that you're seeing a lot of Josh's father. That can't be anything but good for all of you."

If you only knew what happened that night, you'd never say that. "Don't believe everything you hear. Good night, Mary—and thanks."

Her conversation with Mary had only confirmed Toni's belief she should maintain her relationship with David's children, at least until their aunt returned home—or their father came up with a more willing candidate to be their new mommy.

❧

Despite everything that had happened, Toni wanted David to follow through on his promise to bring the children back to Community for Bible study. To let him know he should still do so, Toni decided to call the children and remind them she wanted to see them at church the next day. The telephone at the condo rang four times before David's recorded voice invited her to leave a message.

"This is Toni. I hope you've had a great day today. I'll look for you all at Bible study tomorrow morning."

Her message was short and to the point—and she prayed it would be heeded.

❧

Toni was a few minutes late arriving at Community Church Sunday morning. When she spotted David's truck in the parking lot, she offered a prayer of thanks that he had not let what happened between them keep him and the children from Bible study.

When Toni entered the Seekers class, a discussion about grief was well under way. Without looking at David, she slipped into a chair beside Linda Travers. When one Seeker said he had always heard grief was sinful, Linda pointed out that Jesus was without sin, yet He wept with Mary and Martha over the death of Lazarus.

"Jesus expressed grief at other times too," Greg said. "Let's look at those Scriptures." After a thirty-minute discussion, Greg summarized the main points. "Grief is a normal reaction to tragedy and death, but it doesn't last forever—and God is always there, ready to wipe away every tear."

"If we let Him," said Susan Harmon, Greg's wife. "Some people hold on to their grief until it beats them down and wears them out."

"I like what Psalm 30 verse 5 says about how joy comes in the morning," Linda said.

"That's right, 'weeping may endure for a night, but joy cometh in the morning,' " Greg quoted the King James Version.

"That's it." Linda turned to Toni. "Isn't there an anthem about that?"

"Yes—it's called 'Joy in the Morning.' In fact, the choir is singing it this morning—and I'll be late if I don't go now."

And if I leave now, David won't have to speak to me.

When Toni entered the choir loft and saw David sitting in the congregation with his children, she felt a strange tug at her heart. *They could so easily be my family.* But they weren't. In keeping an old vow, she had refused both David and his children.

Toni stood with the rest of the choir to sing about the heavenly joy that comes in the morning after a night of weeping.

Let David take this message to heart, Lord. He's had more than his share of weeping. It's time for him to reclaim the joy of his salvation.

When Ted Brown had asked Toni to present an offertory solo for that Sunday, she had chosen music that spoke to her own heart. But when she rose to sing that morning, she realized it not only echoed that day's Bible study, but also had a message David needed to hear.

Lord, I thank You for what You have done for me. Help me sing to Your glory.

With Janet Brown accompanying her on the piano, Toni began to sing "A Day of New Beginnings." The words of the song spoke of a new life in Jesus—of God making all things new.

"Amen!" someone said when the last piano note faded.

Amen, Toni's heart echoed.

⤫

Toni did not expect to see David and the children after the service, but they were waiting for her when she emerged from the choir room.

"You sang pretty," Josh said.

"I'm glad you liked it," Toni said.

"That was a cool anthem. I might join the junior choir," Mandy said. "They go on tours and do stuff."

"I never had a chance to do that myself, but it sounds like fun." *And a great way for you to make new friends.*

"We're gonna take a picnic to Soda Park. Come with us, Toni," Josh said.

Toni looked at David. *Is this his idea or yours?*

"Everyone wants you to come," David said pointedly. "We're going home to change clothes. We'll pick you up in twenty minutes."

There you go, giving me orders again. I should say no for that reason alone. But Toni had a reason to go—she needed to have a talk with Josh.

"All right. Can I bring anything?"

"No, thanks. Mrs. Tarpley insisted on doing it all."

⤫

"Slow down, Daddy. We're s'posed to turn off right up there," Josh said when David neared DeSoto State Park's main entrance.

"I know, but the park has over five thousand acres. Today we're going to a place you've never been."

Leaving the truck in a turnout, they hiked down a fairly steep trail. As they went, David pointed out hickory, black and chestnut oaks, pine, poplar, dogwood, and sassafras trees he had learned to identify as a Boy Scout.

At the bottom of the hill, they came to a quiet pool fed by a small waterfall several hundred yards away. With no rain in the last few days, the waterfall was more of a trickle than a torrent, but the pool, outlined by oak leaf hydrangeas and lichen- and moss-covered rocks of all sizes, was beautiful.

"Stay away from that poison oak," David warned. "Those red winterberries are good to eat, but watch out for the thorns."

David set the picnic hamper on a large rock in the clearing. "I hope you like fried chicken and potato salad," he told Toni. "Mrs. Tarpley chose and cooked the menu, and Mandy packed our sodas."

"I put in the cookies," Josh said.

"The ones you didn't eat, that is," Mandy returned.

Toni smiled. *Mandy will always tease her little brother, but she seems much gentler with him, at least.*

After they finished eating, David handed the children small buckets and told them to fill them with small, flat rocks. "I'll teach you how to make them skip across the water later."

"Come on, Josh. I'll help you look. Let's walk down the path and see what we can find," Toni said.

Mandy started to follow them, but David called her back. "You can help me look around here." Toni understood his unspoken message: *I trust you to talk to Josh alone.*

"We can find more, can't we, Toni?" Josh tugged her hand impatiently. "Hurry up!"

Toni let Josh lead her down the path to a place where many small rocks had washed up beside the pool. Josh picked up a few small pebbles, then he found a larger rock and threw it at a nearby tree. A startled blue jay flew from one of the limbs, scolding loudly.

"Pow! Take that, you rat!" Josh picked up an even larger rock, but Toni stayed his hand. "Never throw rocks like that. You almost hit that bird. You could hurt an animal or a person very badly doing that."

Josh dropped the stone and dug the toe of his sneaker into the loamy soil. "I was just playin'. I didn' mean to hurt nothin'."

"I know that, Josh. You weren't thinking just then. But sometimes when you get really mad, you might forget and do things you shouldn't."

Josh looked up at Toni with tears in his eyes. "Cody's daddy says I'm a bad boy."

Toni knelt and put her arms around Josh's thin body. "No, you're not. Getting mad doesn't make you bad, but you should never let the way you feel inside make you do bad things."

"I can't help it," Josh said.

"Yes, you can. When you feel yourself getting mad, just walk away, and nothing bad will happen."

"You mean I should put myself in time-out?"

"Time-out?"

"That's where Miss Mary makes us go when we do something wrong."

"She sends you out of the room?"

"No, there's this special chair in the corner behind a screen. We hafta sit there until we get over bein' bad."

"That's a wonderful idea, Josh—giving yourself a time-out if you get mad. I'm proud of you for figuring that out."

Josh grinned, apparently proud of himself as well. "Hurry up, or Mandy and Daddy'll find more skippin' rocks."

Josh wants to be good, Lord. Help us show him how.

&

"Come on," David called a few moments later. "You should have enough rocks by now."

"I don't know how to do it," Josh said. "Teach me, Daddy."

"Neither do I," Toni admitted.

David demonstrated his skill first by sending a pebble skipping in graceful arcs across the pool. Then he showed each of the children how to hold and throw their stones for maximum distance. Mandy caught on quickly and began to help Josh.

When Toni's first few efforts sank rather than skipped, David put his hand over hers and guided her through the correct motions. Feeling the familiar, almost electrical jolt that accompanied any close contact with David, she moved away.

"Now try it on your own," he said.

The stone hopped once, twice, then sank out of sight. "I guess I don't do very well on my own."

Toni read the question in David's eyes. "Nothing personal, of course," she added.

David glanced toward the children, who had moved some distance away and had their backs to them. Satisfied they were absorbed in skipping stones, he turned to Toni.

"It seems every time we come up here, I manage to upset you."

"I'm not upset."

"Maybe you aren't now, but ever since the other night—"

"I want you to know that Josh and I had a good talk just now," Toni put in before David could say anything else. "I think he really can tell when he's about to lose his temper. He told me he's going to put himself in a time-out when that happens. I think that's real progress. You might want to talk to him about it yourself."

"Thanks. I will. You're so good at handling things like that. I'm not. I'm no good at saying how I feel. What I should have said the other night—what I'm trying to say now—is that the minute I saw you, I knew you were special. Sure, I was glad you and the kids got along, but even if I didn't have them, I'd still want you."

David took her hands in his and spoke slowly. "I love you, Toni, and I want to marry you. For my sake, not theirs."

She felt breathless, as if she had been underwater a long time and needed air. David was looking at her in the familiar, intent way. She now understood its meaning, but it was hard to comprehend that David loved her. When Toni finally managed to speak, her voice was a breathy whisper. "You do?"

David nodded and squeezed her hands. "I know you don't love me yet, but—"

She raised her chin and looked David in the eye. "Who says I don't?"

He looked stunned. "I thought you did."

"I never said that—you assumed it."

David reached out to draw Toni close. "Say it, then."

"You're giving me an order again," she murmured. She pulled back to smile at him. "But in spite of that and everything else, I love you, David."

He kissed her deeply once, then again and again. He finally released Toni with a shout that reverberated through the trees and brought the children running toward them.

Josh's eyes were wide. "What is it, Daddy?"

"Did you see a snake?" Mandy asked anxiously.

"No, kids. That was a happy shout. I want you to meet someone."

He pointed to Toni, and Josh and Mandy exchanged puzzled glances. "We already know Toni," Josh said.

"Yes, but she's going to be Mrs. David Trent. Josh and Mandy—meet your new mommy."

When the meaning of their father's words sank in, Josh grabbed Toni's knees and hung on for dear life, while Mandy gave her a more subdued hug. "I'm so glad," she said.

Josh let go of Toni to jump up and down. "I told everybody I was gonna get a new mommy!" He stood still and looked at Toni. "I'm glad it's not Mrs. Tarpley."

"So am I," David said.

"Amen," added Toni.

And thank You, Lord, for directing all our paths to this day.

epilogue

On a sunny Saturday in early March, after her leisurely exploration of Mexico, Evelyn Trent returned to Rockdale for the first time since Christmas. Evelyn had declared that nothing could keep her from Rockdale when her brother and her former ward exchanged their marriage vows.

David and the children met Evelyn at the Chattanooga airport and took her to her house. Since David had to take Josh and Mandy to their activities that afternoon, David excused himself soon after he brought Evelyn's luggage inside.

"Thirty minutes?" David asked Toni.

"Better make it forty-five."

"What's that all about?" Evelyn asked.

"Our schedules. Sometimes it seems we're going in different directions."

"From what they said on the way home, Josh and Mandy are involved in a lot of different things. I hope they also have time to just be kids."

Toni nodded. "They do. Many of the planned activities revolve around their church groups, and both play seasonal sports. They've made friends and seem happy."

"I see so much difference in the children—and their father—since you came into their lives."

"It's God's work, not mine. Once David realized he could give his guilt and grief to the Lord, he's found real peace. The children's involvement in the church has done wonders for them too."

"That's exactly what I'd hoped. I couldn't be prouder of them—and of you, Toni."

"I had a good role model." Evelyn's praise embarrassed Toni, and she quickly changed the subject. "If you feel up to a short ride, I want to show you something."

"I've already traveled several thousand miles today. I suppose I can handle a few more."

A few minutes later, Toni drove out Rockdale Boulevard, bypassed the gated community near Warren Mountain, and turned onto a street where several new houses were in various stages of construction.

Evelyn expressed her surprise. "When did all this happen? I didn't know anything like this was out here in the woods."

"How could you? You've hardly been here since you retired."

"That's going to change. I've enjoyed all my travels, but I plan to stay home for a long while."

Toni turned into a cul-de-sac and stopped in front of a two-story red brick house at the end of the street. A "SOLD" banner stretched across the builder's sign in the front yard.

"Here we are."

Evelyn gaped, as close to being speechless as Toni had seen her since her retirement dinner. "This is yours?"

Toni nodded. "Ours and Rockdale Federal's."

"David told me when I was here for Christmas you were thinking of building, but he never said a word about this all the way home from the airport."

"That's because the children don't know about it yet. We just closed the deal the day before yesterday, and we want to surprise them."

"I don't know about Josh and Mandy, but you've certainly surprised me."

Toni stopped on the brick walkway and used her hands to sketch their landscaping plans. "I want boxwoods for both sides of the walk. In the beds in front of the house, David will put in azaleas and rhododendrons, butterfly bushes, hydrangeas, and chrysanthemums. This fall, we'll plant lots of daffodil and tulip bulbs."

Evelyn looked amused. "Those are mighty ambitious plans from someone who didn't know a tulip from a toadstool a year ago."

"You can thank David for that. He's been poring over catalogs and trying to teach me a few gardening basics."

"He's always liked digging in the dirt, and I know he missed doing that in the army."

They reached the covered entryway, and Toni unlocked the leaded-paned front door and ushered Evelyn into the stone-tiled foyer.

Evelyn looked into the living and dining rooms flanking the foyer, then her gaze followed the sweep of the spiral stairway. "I had no idea you and David could afford anything so grand."

"Neither did we. We've been looking at houses for several months, but most were either too small or too expensive. David sold construction insurance to the builder. He told David he would reduce the price for a quick sale and accepted our offer."

Toni led Evelyn through the downstairs rooms. "The kitchen is large enough to eat in, and there's a covered porch behind it that we'll screen in. There's the master bedroom— the other three are upstairs."

After walking through the second floor bedrooms and a large room over the garage destined to become the children's playroom, Toni and Evelyn returned to the foyer.

"That was quite a tour. I must say I'm quite impressed by the David Trent mansion," Evelyn said.

Toni smiled. "The Evelyn Trent house once seemed like a mansion to me. Neither David nor I have owned a house before, and we both felt led to this one. We want to make it a true home for Josh and Mandy, and, God willing, any children David and I have together."

"I'm sure it will be. God certainly had a hand in bringing you and David to Rockdale at the right time."

"With a little help from a certain social worker," Toni said.

Evelyn sighed. "You'll always think what you like about that, I suppose. The main thing is you were finally able to rescind your vow to never marry."

"For a long time, I used it as a shield against the pain of what happened to my mother. When I asked God to show me the way I should go, He led me to make a far better vow to David."

"I believe Jean would agree that David couldn't have found a better mother for her children. I'm glad the Websters are coming to the wedding. Josh and Mandy should keep in touch with their mother's family."

"We agree. The children will go to Virginia for a visit this summer."

The doorbell rang, startling them both. Toni opened the door to David, who put his arm around her waist.

"Has Toni shown you around?" he asked Evelyn.

"Yes. It's a beautiful house, and you are both—" Evelyn broke off, choked by sudden emotion.

"We are all truly blessed," David said.

"Amen and amen," added Toni.